Queen
of
Humboldt

Praise for the works of Tagan Shepard

And Then There Was Her

This book really was a joy to read. As soon as I started reading this book I was hooked. I loved the premise. I loved the setting of a winery. There is something so romantic about it, and Shepard writes beautifully so you feel like you can taste the grapes and even feel the soil. I thought all the characters were well done. This was the right book at the right time and it's going on my 2020 favorite list.

-*goodreads*, Lex Kent's Reviews

The romance is very delicately written, a well-balanced slow burn with some spectacularly hot moments too! I could have written thousands of words on how much I love this book, the intricacy of the imagery, how much I want to punch Kacey, and how I can relate to the pain and doubt etched in Madison's soul. Anyone who has ever been made to feel "less than" will be touched by this narrative.

-*NetGalley*, Orlando J.

I adore an age-gap romance, and this slow-burn story is incredibly romantic. There's something about the writing that is lush and elegant and beautiful, and it really suits the story that is set in a gorgeous vineyard. I highly recommend this gorgeous book for anyone looking for an escape.

-*NetGalley*, Karen C.

This book plucked the strings of my romantic side on multiple occasions. I highly recommend this book to the romantics out there and even the aspiring romantics who just need a little encouragement.

-*The Lesbian Review*

Across the Dark Horizon

This is a well written and very fast-paced book. It is not overly long and there is quite a bit of action crammed into the pages. Shepard builds great tension throughout the book through both the plot and the bourgeoning relationship between Charlie and Gail. ...the result is heart-pounding excitement throughout!

-*The Lesbian Review*

Bird on a Wire

This is the second novel by Tagan Shepard. I said for her successful debut that it is a sign that many more fine books are yet to come. I am glad that I was right...With all main elements done well, this makes for another very good book by this author. Keep them coming!

-*goodreads*, Pin's Review

...She has become an author that I will automatically read now. If you are looking for a good drama book with a little romance, give this a read.

-*goodreads*, Lex Reviews

Visiting Hours

...*Visiting Hours* is an emotional tale filled with denial, pain, struggle, commitment, and finally, more than one kind of deep, abiding love.

-*Lambda Literary Review*

About the Author

Tagan Shepard is the author of five novels of sapphic fiction, including the 2019 Goldie winner *Bird on a Wire*. When not writing about extraordinary women loving other extraordinary women she can be found playing video games, reading or sitting in DC Metro traffic.

She lives in Virginia with her wife and two cats.

Queen of Humboldt

Tagan Shepard

BELLA
BOOKS
2020

Bella Books, Inc.
P.O. Box 10543
Tallahassee, FL 32302

Printed in the United States of America on acid-free paper.

First Bella Books Edition 2020

Editor: Cath Walker
Cover Designer: Kayla Mancuso

ISBN: 978-1-64247-156-4

Acknowledgments

While I am generally an author who requires quiet and solitude to write, I took a different path with this book. Major portions were written on glorious Sunday mornings in my local coffee shop, The Raven's Nest in Culpeper, VA. The atmosphere is warm and inviting, the owner is gregarious and has possibly the best memory of any human I've ever met, and the delicious coffee is locally roasted. My sincere thanks for their hospitality. I have missed it greatly during this pandemic.

The writing process is lonely, and I'd never be able to survive it without the wonderful friends I've made in the community. Writing an action novel for the first time presented new and unique challenges. I am indebted to Celeste, Cade, Kate and Andy, the best beta readers anyone could ask for. A special thank you to Carla Chávez for her assistance with Spanish translations. Any mistakes are mine, not hers.

Bella Books is a family. There's no other way to describe it. The love and support I receive from my fellow Bella authors is profound and I am so grateful. Thank you to Cath for her kindness and collaboration as my editor. A simple "thank you" is not enough for Jessica and Linda, but it's what I have to give. You make my dreams come true.

Last but never least, my dearest wife, Cris. Thank you for dealing with my late-night plot ramblings and my early morning character quizzes. You're always my biggest fan and I love you more than I could ever say.

Dedication

As always, to my queen

Author's Note

Human trafficking, particularly the forced labor of Asian and Latinx women and girls, is an international disgrace that deserves more media attention than it currently receives. According to the UN's International Labour Organization (ILO), there were an estimated 40.3 million people being held in modern day slavery in 2016. "Women and girls are disproportionally affected by forced labour, accounting for 99% of victims in the commercial sex industry, and 58% in other sectors." (Global Estimates of Modern Slavery: Forced Labour and Forced Marriage, Geneva, September 2017)

It is imperative for all of us to fight against this exploitation. In the United States there are several organizations that are available to help if you or someone you know is aware of potential human trafficking situations:

National Human Trafficking Hotline 1-888-373-7888
humantraffickinghotline.org

Polaris Project polarisproject.org

CAST (Coalition to Abolish Slavery & Trafficking)
castla.org

In light of the recent attention paid to white authors co-opting the stories of People of Color, I want to be transparent. I am a white author and Marisol Soltero is a Latinx character. This is a story with a Latinx lead, it is not a story about *being* Latinx. Her experience as a Latinx-American is something I can never understand, but I will do my best to tell the story of her actions, her passions and her love. Because of the absence of government support, minority communities, including the LGBTQ community, have always helped ourselves. Women in particular have been those on the front lines and I want to honor that tradition with Marisol, putting herself in danger to protect her community.

I encourage everyone who reads this book to also read Own Voices stories by LGBTQ Latinx authors. My personal recommendations are *Lex Files* by Celeste Castro and *Blanca & Roja* by Anna-Marie McLemore.

PROLOGUE

2010

Marisol lay back, content to let Sabrina do all the work. Her view from the nest of pillows was almost as delicious as the sensations Sabrina's work was creating. Their legs were entwined, smooth pale white and lean red-brown glistening with sweat in the morning sun. Sabrina's hips tipped forward, mixing Marisol's raven black curls with her deep auburn. She moaned low in her chest and grabbed at Marisol's hips, her eyes closed as she moved faster.

She tipped her head back and screamed as her tension broke, and Marisol yelled right along with her, her own voice an octave lower than Sabrina's high, delighted soprano. In just three short days they had attuned their bodies perfectly. Pulses of pleasure rippled through Marisol as Sabrina continued to rock against her, her movements slower and more languid after her release.

Sabrina slowed and stilled, her sweat-soaked body collapsing against Marisol. Once she was down in the pile of pillows, her chest heaving, Marisol was on the move, laying a trail of kisses across Sabrina's face and neck as she slipped her body on top.

She nipped at the tip of her collarbone, a spot she'd learned last night was ticklish, earning a giggle and playful shove. Her kisses moved further down. As she passed over Sabrina's ample breasts the giggling died and her breathing deepened. Lower still and Sabrina's long, sure fingers snaked into the short strands of Marisol's damp hair. Her first taste of the morning had Sabrina panting.

"Mmmm," she hummed. "Don't stop. Please don't stop."

Marisol had no intention of stopping. She wrapped her arms around Sabrina's thighs and redoubled her efforts, Sabrina groaning above her. The groan lengthened into a moan which ended in a shout, her hands fisting in Marisol's hair.

Flopping onto her back and tossing away some of the ridiculous number of pillows, Marisol pulled Sabrina to her. She was still breathing hard from her last release. Marisol had discovered Sabrina liked to be held as she came down. Sabrina curled against her side, spreading her palm over the spot between her breasts where Marisol's heart pounded. Marisol put her hand on top of Sabrina's making her smile and look up with dreamy, glassy eyes.

"I could get used to this," Sabrina said, her voice languid and her eyes drooping.

"It was one of the better weekends I've had in a while."

"Ugh, don't remind me it's over."

"There's another one coming soon."

Sabrina's eyes were clearer now, meeting Marisol's. "So you…want to do this again next weekend?"

There was hope in her voice, poorly hidden behind a forced casualness. Marisol pushed her own anticipation down, all too aware that hope had never brought her anything good. "I don't have any plans."

Sabrina didn't respond, just smiled and laid her head back down on Marisol's shoulder, their joined hands resting on Marisol's heart.

They both had to get ready for work, so Marisol declined a shower in the hotel. After all, their one-night stand had stretched from Friday night to Saturday morning when Marisol had joined Sabrina in the shower. The same had happened

Sunday morning. As nice as third repeat would be, she had an appointment.

Marisol refused a lift back to the bar to collect her Harley, preferring a brisk morning walk. Its handlebars were peppered with parking tickets, which she tossed into the nearest trash can before speeding across town to shower and change.

She snagged one of the last spots on the top level of the parking deck across from the George N. Leighton Criminal Courthouse. Crossing the lot, she spotted a familiar white SUV and stopped in the process of calling the elevator to watch the driver's door open. What Marisol wore today wasn't her usual and felt strange on her skin. Her tailored slacks didn't fit like her leather pants, but at least the shirt was from the men's section and the leather blazer smelled like her motorcycle jacket. Watching a very familiar pair of legs emerge from the SUV made her clothes feel all the more uncomfortable. All weekend those legs had been wrapped around her naked body and her body yearned to be naked again at the sight of them.

"Marisol?" Sabrina squeaked, her sharp heels skidding to a stop.

"Good morning," Marisol said, then let one side of her lips twitch up. "Again."

Sabrina looked much as she had when they'd met at the bar Friday night. Her skirt suit, professional haircut and sensible shoes had reminded Marisol of a lawyer then. The assessment seemed even more accurate now.

"What are you doing here?" Sabrina asked as the elevator doors slid open.

"Holding the elevator," she replied.

"Of course." Sabrina looked her over from head to toe, her tongue peeking out to catch her upper lip. "I don't think it would've left me, though. The elevators here are really slow."

"Are they? I've only been here once before." The doors jerked shut and the gears groaned into life. "You come here often?"

Sabrina's perfume had Marisol's head spinning with the scent of lily and peach. So did the way she laughed and looked away.

"Sorry," Marisol replied, her own smile widening. "That sounded like a line, didn't it?"

"And not even the best one you've used on me," she said. Her eyes wandered again and she caught her bottom lip between her teeth. "Journalist?"

"Is it that obvious?" Marisol waved a hand over her meticulously bland outfit. They hadn't gotten around to exchanging trivial information like professions or even last names.

"It's not the clothes," Sabrina responded as the elevator ground past another floor. "It's the knack for setting your audience at ease."

"So you're at ease?"

Sabrina's purposeful hesitation was as good as affirmation. "To answer your question, I haven't come here often, but it'll be a regular stop from now on."

"Ah," Marisol leaned in. "Lawyer."

"Is it that obvious?"

The doors opened and Marisol held them back for her. "It isn't the clothes. It's the knack of making your audience nervous."

She laughed and Marisol forgot all about the courthouse and the asshole waiting inside and the cops milling around like fleas on a dog's back. They both looked at the imposing structure across the street and then around them, as if searching for a reason not to cross the pavement.

"Well, I should warn you it'll be a long day," Sabrina said, indicating the coffee shop next door with a jerk of her head. "You should probably fortify yourself."

"Only if you let me buy you a cup."

Sabrina pulled the door open and said over her shoulder, "I'll even sit with you while you drink it."

Marisol usually only drank the thick, deliciously bitter brew from her local Puerto Rican bodega, but she'd drink mud to spend more time with Sabrina. She watched the easy way Sabrina ordered for them both, the way she commanded the room effortlessly. It had been that confidence that had attracted Marisol, though she'd been at the bar on Friday night to study the crowd in preparation for her role today, not to pick up a beautiful woman. Sabrina had a way of making her forget everything she was supposed to do and everyone she was supposed to be.

While she waited for their lattes, Marisol considered the new knowledge that Sabrina was an attorney. It would complicate matters, but she did want to see Sabrina again and she knew all about complicated. She could make it work. All she had to do was win her over before she found out the truth.

"Mind if we drink these while we walk? I'm meeting someone outside the courthouse and I don't want to keep them waiting."

"Should I be jealous?" Marisol asked. She tried to make it playful, but she felt the words gnaw at the pit of her stomach.

Sabrina turned to her while they waited at the crosswalk. She took a sip of her coffee, leaving a pale-rose lip print on the lid. Marisol had washed a similar print off her inner thigh during one of her many showers at the hotel.

"Krone's a colleague and old enough to be my father."

A tiny voice in the back of Marisol's head told her this conversation was a bad idea, but she ignored it. She was only halfway through the coffee and she was ready to take risks with this woman.

"Are you here for a particular case, or are you covering a beat?" Sabrina asked.

The question reminded Marisol she was playing a part and she slipped back into it reluctantly. "I'm freelance. Hoping to find something worth writing about today. Want to give me any tips?"

"Oh no," Sabrina said, swirling her paper cup. "I can't talk about my cases."

"Defense attorney?"

"God no," she replied, her face hardening. "I couldn't imagine helping a guilty person go free. I mean—don't get me wrong—I believe everyone has the right to a fair trial…"

"You'd just rather be on the good side."

"Exactly."

"And what about the wrongfully accused?"

"I'd never send an innocent man to prison."

There was such sincerity in her words, Marisol was inclined to believe her. She couldn't help thinking of the prosecutor at her own trial. He'd taken far too much joy in sending her away. Of course, she'd been guilty of everything she'd been convicted of and more.

The light changed and Sabrina started forward with the crowd. She must be the new Assistant State's Attorney Marisol had heard about. As if things weren't complicated enough. She should let it go—keep the memory of a lovely weekend and disappear into the crowd. Instead, she hurried to catch up and leaned close to Sabrina's ear.

"Like you said, Brin, it'll be a long day. I'll need a drink after. Maybe even dinner."

Sabrina's smile answered before she did. "Brin? Hmm. I like that. We'll discuss dinner over the first drink."

When they made it to the courthouse stairs, a man in an off-the-rack suit waved his arm and Sabrina waved back. Turning to Marisol she said, "There's Krone. So, Mario's? Six thirty?"

Marisol nodded and Sabrina hurried away. As she made her way into the crowd surging up the stairs, Marisol caught the man's confused glare in her direction. He pointed at her and Sabrina's frowning gaze turned to follow.

Making herself comfortable in the pool of reporters at the back of the courtroom, Marisol pulled out a notepad and started doodling while the room filled. Sabrina marched in, her eyes straight ahead, but her colleague was looking into every face. When he finally found Marisol, he smirked and she smirked right back. He whispered in Sabrina's ear but she didn't react. It was the lack of response that had Marisol's gut twisting.

The judge arrived fifteen minutes late, looking bored. He addressed Sabrina as Assistant State's Attorney Sloane, confirming the trouble Marisol had gotten herself into. As the day progressed Marisol's notepad filled with doodles. Men in orange jumpsuits filed in and out of the room. Marisol stopped squirming after the third one. She remembered all too well what it felt like to be shackled wrist and ankle. Her jumpsuit had smelled like beef stew and had made her itch all over.

Sabrina threw the book at most of the violent offenders. Anyone who had used a gun, Marisol noticed, earned a higher bail. In contrast, the nonviolent offenders, particularly petty drug offenses or the obviously destitute, were shown a shocking amount of leniency. Marisol wondered if Sabrina would be so kind in this new role after she'd been burned a few times.

By the time Marisol's mark shuffled into the room, she already knew he wouldn't be walking free. Marisol had come to court to assess the new prosecutor, fully prepared to take matters into her own hands if she thought the law wouldn't exact justice, but she needn't have bothered. No way Sabrina would be lenient with him, given his crimes. This day had been a waste, but she waited it out anyway. His face was smug and his lawyer was exactly the sort of clown Sloane had described over lattes. She barely gave him a chance to speak. His client went back to jail, his unattainable bond the least of his worries with a prosecutor like that on his case. Marisol could've left the courtroom, knowing she could leave her target's punishment to ASA Sloane. Another abuser off the street, even if it took the coke Marisol planted on him to put him away. A few familiar faces hurried out, shaking their heads and no doubt writing off their colleague for good. She didn't leave though. She waited until the end of the docket when even the judge looked exhausted.

As the crowd hurried for the doors, Marisol watched Sloane pack her bag. She didn't look tired, but strain pulled at her eyes. Sloane looked over her shoulder once, her eyes meeting Marisol's. The lightness that had been there that morning was gone. She looked at Marisol the way she'd looked at all the men in orange jumpsuits.

Even though she knew she'd be drinking alone, hope took her to the bar at Mario's at six thirty. She drank beer at first, then switched to tequila. By the time the kitchen closed Marisol was slumped in her seat. She looked at the door every time it opened, but Sloane never walked through. When the bar closed she called a cab rather than risk a DUI. While she waited on the curb she looked into the high-rise apartment buildings around her, wondering if Sabrina Sloane was pacing behind one of the lit windows.

CHAPTER ONE

Ten Years Later

The dance floor moved like a living creature, a hive of humanity swaying and gyrating in unison to the techno bass line. The lighting was dim and blue, with white spotlights flickering across the crowd, illuminating flashes of skin. The mob jumped and danced in harmony, the unified ecstasy palpable through the semidarkness.

The band finished in an electronic crescendo and the crowd roared their approval. The singers, a threesome of indistinguishable blondes in tight dresses and wild makeup, bowed and filed off the stage. The club's sound system picked up with a similar track at a lower volume. As some of the crowd made their way to the bar, Marisol Soltero returned her attention to the redhead draped across her lap.

"You havin' a good time, baby?" the woman asked as she dove again for Marisol's neck.

She was drunk and sloppy and drooling all over Marisol's leather jacket, but she was warm and that was enough these days. She didn't bother to answer. Marisol guessed she was in her early twenties, so she probably didn't care about much beyond having a good time and getting laid. Marisol had had the same priorities then. Now at forty, she had other concerns, but the distraction wasn't unwelcome.

Marisol gripped hard at the redhead's miniskirt, pulling the woman toward her, enjoying the way bare legs slid along her leather pants. She squeaked with pleasure and redoubled her efforts to leave her saliva on every inch of Marisol's exposed skin, her hands roaming freely under Marisol's leather jacket. It didn't take long for her to bore Marisol, who let her attention wander to her club.

Club Alhambra, nestled in the heart of Humboldt Park in Chicago's West Side, was Marisol's center of operations. Her place to see and be seen. Where her clients, rich and poor, could mingle and make her a fortune. She'd gutted and remodeled an old 1920s theatre and made it into her sanctuary. The stage was original, if shortened significantly to provide a larger dance floor. The mezzanine was a massive bar and everything above remained as before, private seating for the rich and famous. Marisol charged outrageous rates for the privilege of renting a box and the compulsory bottle service.

Of course Marisol's box was the best. It was massive, comprised of two boxes from the original design. Deep leather couches and polished marble tables surrounded by wingback chairs filled the space. She had the best view from here—the width and breadth of the dance floor and the length of the bar. She could see every entrance and exit. More importantly, everyone could see her. It was the one area of the club that was well lit and the speakers were turned low. The thumping bass line was ever present here, but the rest was a hollow echo.

Most people called Marisol's box The Throne Room. Admittance was by invitation only. Everyone kept an eye on The Throne Room, hoping they were cool enough, sexy enough or rich enough to catch Marisol's attention. Most of them, like the redhead whose attentions were now an annoyance, had no idea what to do with themselves if they ever got up here.

Marisol caught the eye of her bodyguard, Gray. He was a lumbering, massive specimen, his muscles straining the seams on his tailored suit and his bald head gleaming in the orange glow of the lights. He looked like a meathead, but his eyes were sharp and his mind even sharper. She cut her eyes toward a nearby table where an unconscious occupant's face was plastered to the marble next to a half-finished line of cocaine.

Gray took a phone out of his breast pocket as he walked across the room. He snapped pictures from several different angles before hauling the guy up by the armpits. He was so stoned his head lolled around on his neck as Gray dragged him out. A minute later, Marisol's phone buzzed.

"Take a break, *cariño*," Marisol said, removing the girl from her lap.

Far from being upset, the redhead helped herself to some fine añejo tequila while Marisol checked her phone. Gray had an eye for staging. Unfortunately for Judge Marshall, his adult son wasn't careful about where he snorted coke. Marisol filed the photos for another day when they would have more value.

Gray made it back to The Throne Room just in time to intercept a gate-crasher in the form of Twitchy D, a tweaker who had worked for Marisol until he started smoking more meth than he could handle. The usual punishment was a trip to the bottom of the Chicago River, but she took pity on a longtime employee. He was thin and tall, with gangly arms and erratic movements. His stringy, curly hair always looked like he had just showered, but his body certainly didn't smell like it.

Twitchy D turned his manic gaze on Marisol as Gray stopped him with a hand on his chest. His eyes held a desperate glee that intrigued Marisol, so she waved him over. Gray kept a close eye on him as he shuffled over, hopping along like a marionette caught in a windstorm. He cut a glance at the coke Judge Marshall's wayward son had abandoned on the table, a weaselly giggle bursting from his lips.

Marisol waited until his eyes focused on her before she asked, "What're you doin' here, D?"

"Got some info, Your Majesty." Words burst out of him in a rush. "There's a new gang trying to push into your turf. Got a big thing goin' down tonight."

Gray shook him by the shoulder and his whole body flopped around like a rag doll. "Don't be an idiot, D. No one's stupid enough to move in on Marisol."

The last group to challenge her dominance had been skinheads calling themselves The Moscow Mules. Six years earlier they had roughed up the local bodegas for protection money. Marisol had visited their leader at his biker bar hangout and had politely informed him he had exactly three days to move his men along. Three days and one hour later, when they had still been in place, she came down on them like fire from heaven. No one had come near her territory since, earning her the title The Queen of Humboldt.

"I know!" D said, giggling and picking at a sore on his cheek. "That's why I came to tell you first! So you could take care of them. You know I'm loyal. I want you to destroy them." His eyes went to the cocaine again. "Tonight."

"You know I watch my borders, D," Marisol said, drumming her fingers on her own leather-clad thigh. "Closest gang with any clout's in Fuller Park."

"Not moving on Humboldt yet. That would be suicide." His shoulder shot up and back down again seemingly of its own accord. The movement caught his eye, dragging his attention from Marisol so his next words were mumbled into his shirt. "Gotta get themselves on the map first. That's what tonight's about."

Marisol snapped her fingers, regaining his focus. "What's happening tonight, D?"

"Something big." His anemic tongue slid over his cracked lips. "They're going to take her out."

"Take who out?"

"That tight ass little governor of ours. Getting too tough on crime, they said. Need to send a message." He giggled and put his fingertips in his mouth, saying his next words around dirty fingernails. "Shame. She's a hot one."

Marisol's jaw tightened. She held still as she spoke. "Tell me."

"She's coming to Chicago tonight. Left the capital late, but she's on her way here. They're gonna get her in her apartment. Not much security there and anyone can deal with the state pigs."

1115 Riverview. Apartment 30GH. One doorman and a geriatric rent-a-cop who could be overpowered by a determined house cat. But they wouldn't have Chicago city cops to deal with. The Governor's security detail of Illinois State Police officers would put up more of a fight, but how many would she have with her? The Governor, no matter where she was, was the jurisdiction of the State Police.

"Who?" When D didn't answer the question, Marisol sat forward and said louder, "Who are they, D?"

He shrugged, chewing on his nails.

Marisol sat back, throwing her arm around the redhead and dragging her close. "Gold Coast isn't my territory."

Panic flooded Twitchy D's eyes. She watched him register his reward slipping away. "They're after the whole city. This is just a first strike. They'll be after you next."

Marisol looked at Gray, who had perfected a stoically neutral expression and was using it now. She looked back at Twitchy D, searching his face for a lie. After a moment, she jerked her head toward the table. Gray released him and D attacked the surface with glee.

"Why don't you go get a drink, *cariño?*"

"Got one," the redhead said, reaching for Marisol's tequila again.

Gray caught her wrist. He jabbed his thumb over his shoulder and she hurried off. When she was out of earshot, he leaned in close and said, "Twitchy D isn't a reliable source. Everyone knows he's out of his mind half the time."

"Which is why he hears more than he should."

"It's none of our concern, boss."

Scanning the crowd at the bar, Marisol spotted a dark-skinned Marine in full uniform, her ponytail wrapped in a bun at the base of her neck. She nursed a beer, her eyes darting up to Marisol's Throne Room often enough to be obvious. "No, it isn't."

"It would be nice though," Gray mused, rubbing his chin. "She's been on our asses for years. Having her out of the way and our hands clean will make our lives a lot easier."

Moving to the balcony railing, Marisol watched the Marine raise a toast with a few uniformed buddies. When she turned her eyes back to the Throne Room to find Marisol watching her, she choked on her beer.

Twitchy D fell out of his chair with a muffled crash.

"Damn that guy." Gray turned back to Marisol. "We can decide about this after I get rid of him."

"There's nothing to decide, Gray." She looked back into the crowd, noticing several pairs of eyes on her. That would complicate things. She looked back to the Marine. "I think I'll go have some fun."

He followed her gaze and shook his head. Marisol knew he wouldn't be fooled, and his words carried an icy warning. "I'm serious. We should stay out of it, boss. See what happens tonight and go from there. Or, better yet, turn D over to the cops after she's toast."

The Marine was looking up at Marisol every few seconds. The way she was laughing along with her friends looked forced, like she wasn't hearing anything they said. Marisol straightened and slapped Gray on the shoulder.

"That's a good plan," she said, descending into the crowd.

Music wrapped around her as she stalked through the dance floor, the masses parting for her. Though she saw hunger on more than one face, her patrons were too well-behaved to approach unsolicited. The Marine's eyes continuously flicked over to Marisol as if drawn to her body. One look. That was all it would take. She would give the Marine one look and she would follow Marisol anywhere.

The soldiers were the only ones who held their ground as Marisol approached, though her Marine looked ready to faint. Marisol stepped close enough to smell cheap beer and expensive perfume. She let herself wonder for a moment what this woman would look like out of that starched collar and those gleaming shoes. She had every opportunity to find out, but she knew she didn't have time.

When she felt the Marine's breath on her cheek, Marisol captured her with a long, smoldering look and watched her shudder. Only one woman she'd ever met had been able to resist Marisol's cobra-like eyes. Just as she suspected, the Marine's breathing hitched and she licked her lips.

Without a word, Marisol walked away. She went past the long line for the men's room and the longer line for the women's room, stopping at a guarded entrance marked "Private". She spoke a few words into the guard's ear before continuing around the velvet rope. At the end of a dark corridor stood another bathroom, this one deserted. Slipping inside, Marisol washed her hands and neck, removing all trace of the redhead.

It wouldn't take long for Angel to extend Marisol's invitation to the Marine, and not much longer for her friends to convince her to accept. She'd be here in moments and Marisol needed to be gone. Pushing aside the painting of a Spanish landscape, Marisol flipped the switch for the hidden door. Slipping through, she pulled it shut just in time to hear the bathroom door open. She was in the alley a moment later, sliding onto the seat of her motorcycle.

If she'd read the Marine correctly, she wouldn't tell her friends she'd entered an empty bathroom. Disappointment and confusion would keep her hidden there long enough to convince the others Marisol had given her the night of her life. That was all the alibi Marisol needed.

CHAPTER TWO

Tires hummed as they sped down the highway, their whine accompanied by the click of Governor Sabrina Sloane's fingernails over her keyboard. The man and woman across from her focused on their cell phones, their eyes flicking up to the windows each time a set of headlights flashed by. The third officer, seated beside her with his beefy arm drawn as far from her as possible, didn't even muster that much enthusiasm. They never looked at her and she rarely looked at them. She tried to be personable, but she hadn't grown accustomed to travelling with bodyguards in the two years since her election and she doubted she ever would.

When her phone rang, Sloane ignored it until she finished typing. The police officers exchanged an unreadable look and Sloane finally picked up the call.

"Sloane."

"It's more becoming to answer a call with your full name and title, Madame Governor."

Forcing her lips into a smile, she replied, "It's my personal line, Lily. I assume my friends and family know who I am."

"This is your state-issued cell, Governor."

Scrunching her eyebrows together, Sloane took the phone from her ear to examine it. Sure enough, the plain black case bore a tag denoting it "Property of the State of Illinois".

"Right you are, Lily. Give me a moment to switch to my headset."

Sloane caught the tail end of Lily's snicker through her earpiece and chose to let it go. Now that her hands were free, she went back to her laptop.

Lily didn't wait for confirmation that Sloane was listening. "I've rescheduled your call with the Ethics Committee."

"Why would you do that?"

"Because you scheduled it for tomorrow."

"And?"

"And tomorrow is Saturday."

"Is that supposed to answer my question? Who's unavailable?"

"You are unavailable." Age had given Lily's voice the crackle of dried leaves but had not lessened its authoritative ring. "I've scheduled your massage for tomorrow afternoon at twelve. Your manicurist will arrive at ten and should be done in time."

"I don't need a massage or a manicure," Sloane said, pausing her typing long enough to note that, strictly speaking, she was wrong. "I need to ensure my administration…"

"Your administration is beyond reproach. Your cuticles, however…"

"Lily…"

Her assistant plowed on, "I've rescheduled your dentist appointment. Again. I had to assure Dr. Holmes that you're flossing. Please don't make a liar of me."

Sloane slammed the lid of her laptop closed. "That's enough nagging, Lily."

"Not quite," she replied. "The Ethics Committee will meet with you in Springfield Monday at eight a.m. You have an interview with Channel Three at nine in your office. I've allowed them two hours and sent along the standard list of restricted questions."

"I have no restricted questions."

"They always ask for a list and they're annoying when I tell them there isn't one. I appease them with a memo full of mumbo jumbo."

The car slowed and the click of the turn signal joined the white noise. The officers put away their phones, their eyes scanning the downtown Chicago skyline. Sloane slipped her laptop into her bag and turned her full attention to her assistant.

"What about my schedule for Sunday?"

"I recommend a visit to Holy Name Cathedral. It's never too early to think about reelection."

"I'm focused on governing at the moment. What's on my schedule?"

"Miss Ford is coming by for lunch at eleven thirty. I've blocked off two hours."

"I doubt she'll stay two hours."

"So just lunch this time."

Sloane turned her head, attempting to hide her blush from the three officers. She suspected they knew the arrangements she had with certain friends just as Lily did, but she didn't want to discuss her romantic liaisons in front of them. "What else?"

"Call with Governor Hill of Indiana at two. The Attorney General at three."

"Is something wrong?"

"He's concerned about a bill under consideration in the Senate. I've emailed a memo."

Fighting the urge to grab her laptop, she said, "I'll check it when I get settled. What else?"

"Nothing if you intend to make it back to Springfield at a reasonable hour, but the Democratic Party would like to consult on the next election."

The State Senate was up for grabs again in November and there was every chance they'd earn the largest majority since the 1930s. Her resumé as State's Attorney and a campaign focused on law and order made her popular enough to bring in swing voters. Her record on social issues and her own sexuality made her beloved among the party faithful. Sloane regarded campaigning as a waste of time that should be spent legislating, but if she could help some of the first-time candidates on the ticket, she'd hand over a few hours.

"Schedule a call at four."

The limo pulled to a stop in front of her building and Officer Bates jumped out of the passenger's seat to head inside. Sloane ground her teeth as she waited to be allowed out. It irked her that Bates would be searching her condo while she waited helplessly at the curb, but it was a concession her security team had insisted upon since they weren't allowed in her home after the initial search. Considering that she had forced them to occupy an apartment three floors below her own when she was in town, they wouldn't budge on this one precaution.

"So you'll be leaving Chicago at five?"

"I should eat before I leave so I can work when I get back. Make it six."

"That's an excellent idea. Shall I have Mario's send dinner over?"

"Absolutely not."

"Terroir?"

"Too fancy. Just get me a salad from somewhere?"

"Of course. Enjoy your weekend, Governor Sloane."

Bates reappeared and opened her door as Sloane replied, "You too, Lily. Thank you."

Sloane's blue dress was form-fitting to mid-calf, forcing her to twist awkwardly to exit the limo. An officer collected her blazer and laptop bag, carrying them with one hand while keeping the other on her back. His eyes never stopped moving while they were in public, so she waited until they were safely in the elevator before asking for her blazer. The evening chill pimpled her bare arms, making her regret the sleeveless, high neck dress.

"I forgot my luggage." Sloane tried to turn back, but the officers flanking her kept her moving forward.

"Rogers will bring it after he parks," one of them said.

She looked at his face, trying to remember his name. He was relatively new, but she made it a point to know everyone on her team. She wanted to reprimand him for treating her like a child, but she was sure he had the best intentions. It wasn't worth yet another fight with the State Police.

"Thank him for me, would you?"

"Yes, ma'am."

The engine behind them roared to life as the guards hustled Sloane inside. She watched the limo pull away from the curb as the four of them crowded into the elevator. A hot bath and her own bed were waiting a short ride away.

CHAPTER THREE

The matte-black Ducati 1299 roared up to the curb and Marisol scanned the street and surrounding windows before killing the engine. Chicago's upper crust occupied this stretch of high-rise condos and none of them would care what happened in this deserted alley. They were the type that never looked down to notice those they stepped on. Still, Marisol was only alive because she was cautious.

When she was sure the street was clear, she swung her leg over the bike. It cut her to leave it here, her pride and joy, but crime on the Gold Coast was white-collar, not car theft.

Like the bike, Marisol's clothing rendered her invisible. The supple black leather pants hugged her muscular legs but gave her range of motion. The same was true of the simple, dark gray V-neck T-shirt and leather motorcycle jacket. She wore her black hair cropped close at the back and sides but with long bangs that covered one eye. Vanity had made her color her hair when gray started to appear, but the shade was her natural one. Her eyes were a rich, earthy brown and sunk deep in her long, thin face. Her skin was a similar shade, but with a redder hue. Her features were an asset on a night like this, allowing her to blend with liquid ease into the shadows.

Slipping along the wall to avoid the glow of a nearby street lamp, Marisol made her way to the rear service entrance for number 1115. Pulling up an app on her phone, she keyed in her password and cycled through camera feeds.

"Come on. Come on," she whispered, checking the streets again.

Finally, the image switched to the one she wanted—the other side of this door and hallway beyond. Finding it empty, she keyed in the security code from memory. It chirped approval and the door clicked open. The roar of an engine hurried her, and she caught a glimpse of a very familiar limousine rolling down the street as she slipped inside.

She ran down the hall, her heavy boots thudding on the tile floor, her eyes on her phone. Occasionally she saw herself streak across the screen, but she knew she was the only one monitoring the feeds right now. If she was too late, she could always wipe the cameras' memory.

Two doors loomed into her vision, forcing her into a quick decision. The service elevator doors were open, so she wouldn't have to wait, but the elevator was an old, lumbering model. The other door led to the maintenance staircase. Marisol was fit, in fact she was almost obsessive about working out, but thirty flights of stairs was a lot for anyone.

In the end the open elevator doors won. She slammed her palm into the button for the twenty-ninth floor before she was fully inside the car. As the doors closed with surprising speed she returned her focus to her phone, leaving the ground level cameras in favor of those for the thirtieth floor. When she'd hacked the building's security system several years ago its disorganization had appalled her. She'd had to build this app to make sense of the different feeds. It wasn't hard, but it was irritating, and she was shocked no one had found her yet.

The thirtieth-floor feeds were as deserted as all the others, so she switched back to the twenty-ninth floor, her destination.

The elevators required key fob recognition to access the top floor. The risk in stealing or spoofing a fob had been too great, so she needed a different route to Sloane's floor. Fortunately, the air ducts in this old building were huge.

The cameras went through three cycles of empty halls and closed doors before Marisol left the elevator. Confident that her path to the utility room was clear, she switched back to the cameras for thirty. Movement at last. She saw the elevator lights come to life on her phone before she swapped her phone for the lock-pick set. The tumblers creaked as the door groaned open.

"You should oil your locks," Marisol whispered into the darkened utility room.

She crossed the room without turning on the lights. The elevator's gears rattled, covering the sound of her removing the grate from the air duct. She'd just slipped inside the metal tube when the elevator stopped.

"Shit," she growled, picking up her pace as she army-crawled through the duct.

She shimmied up, bracing herself on the seams with elbows and knees. Sweat popped out on her forehead as she climbed the vertical section. Muffled shouting filtered through the grates ahead. Marisol crawled faster, her feet banging the metal surface, creating too much noise. She heard the bark of authoritative male voices.

With fifty feet to go, she heard the first gunshot. Marisol forgot caution and dragged her body through the duct. The first shot was followed by a flurry of others. A stray bullet tore a hole in the grate ahead, throwing a spotlight into the dusty air. The shots popped like firecrackers, but there were fewer and fewer as the seconds passed.

Marisol reached the grate and slammed her joined wrists into the flimsy metal. It buckled, tumbling to the thick, royal blue carpet below. Marisol pulled herself after it, landing on top and rolling forward, coming to a rest on one knee, her outstretched hands cradling her chrome-plated Colt M1911.

Her eyes darted around the hall, assessing the scene. Two men in the trademark nondescript black suits of bodyguards lay face down on the floor, their pooling blood ruining the carpet. A woman in a similar, if better-tailored, suit sat against the wall, her wrist twisted at her side and her vacant eyes staring through Marisol.

Governor Sabrina Sloane knelt in the corner, one hand thrown up to block her view of the pistol pointed at her left eye. The woman holding the gun wore all black, her face smeared with black grease and a stocking cap covering her hair. A sneer twisted her features as she spun, turning her weapon on the new threat.

Marisol squeezed the trigger three times in quick succession, painting the wall behind the assassin's ruined head in a macabre design. Before the body fell, Marisol was up and running. Her chest clenched at how close she had come to being too late. She packed away that emotion with all her others and hauled Sloane roughly to her feet. Her eyes were dull with shock. A tinny, distant chatter came from the device jammed into the dead assassin's ear.

"Move!" hissed Marisol.

She pushed Sloane past the bodies of her guards toward the elevator. It dinged open the moment Marisol hit the button and she shoved Sloane inside. To her credit, the Governor recovered from her near-death experience quickly.

She glared with naked suspicion at Marisol. "What are *you* doing here?"

Before Marisol had a chance to answer, two men appeared in front of the elevator doors. Their clothes were black and their faces smeared with black like the assassin's. The one on the right smirked, his lip curling up to reveal a chipped incisor, and raised a strange looking gun. Her first instinct was to slide her body sideways, blocking Sloane from his view and aim, and that instinct was her downfall. The gun emitted a quiet pop and a blur of red. Rather than the explosive agony of the bullet she'd been expecting, there was a stabbing pain and a burning sensation under her skin. She cried out in shock and pain, looking down to see a dart the length of her palm lodged in her chest. Wrenching the dart out, she doubled over as the burning sensation spread.

"Two? What the fuck?"

"I don't fucking know just shoot her!"

There was another pop and hiss followed by a pained shriek from Sloane. The sound seared through Marisol's mind and she whipped her head up in time to see the elevator doors sliding into motion and the two men facing off at each other.

"Not the dart, dumbass, shoo…"

Marisol's Colt stopped him midsentence. She turned her gun on the other man, though the movement sent another searing wave of pain under her skin. She fired two bullets into his chest and had time to watch his mouth form a perfect circle and his body tip backward before the doors slid shut and the elevator zipped down toward the lobby.

Sloane's cry was dying down, but she scrabbled at the dart in her shoulder. Marisol wrenched it free and pressed her hand over the spot of blood it had left on her dress. The dart was a simple metal tube with a feathery end on one side and a large barb on the other, beneath which was a short hypodermic needle.

"Let go of me," Sloane roared, pushing Marisol's arm off her and backing into the farthest corner. "What is going on?"

Marisol ejected the Colt's magazine and replaced it with a fresh one. She didn't know what was waiting for them in the lobby, but she wanted to be fully loaded for whatever it was.

"People were sent to kill you. I killed them. You're welcome."

"I need a little more explanation than that, Marisol Soltero. Stop this elevator immediately. I'm not going anywhere with a criminal."

She spoke with well-bred contempt and Marisol cringed at the tone. "Back off and shut up if you're interested in living, Governor."

"You won't get away with this. What did you inject me with?"

Marisol was wondering the same thing herself, but her mind chose that moment to lurch. She shook her head, trying to clear it, but it only became more muddled. She looked down at the pair of darts on the floor, but the floor wobbled and so did her knees.

"Whatever you think you…"

Marisol held up her hand and Sloane's teeth snapped shut. Whatever had been in the dart was making her left arm tingle. She flexed her hand but the simple motion took all her concentration.

Beside her, Sloane stumbled and uttered a soft "Oh."

Marisol's body ached all over and cold spread through her muscles. Unbidden, images from nature documentaries flashed through her mind. Tigers with their tongues lolling out as zookeepers ran tests. Polar bears stumbling across frozen landscapes while scientists trailed slowly behind, waiting for their tranquilizers to take effect. *Tranquilizer darts.*

"Fuck."

Marisol yanked her jacket off as sweat popped out on her brow. She grabbed Sloane by the shoulder as she stumbled again, holding her body close and upright.

"Don't move," Marisol growled. "Hold still and the drug will take longer to move through your system."

Sloane's fingers scratched at her once, but then she fell to her knees. Marisol fell too and, while she would've preferred to think it was to keep Sloane from falling on her face, she knew it was the drug. It was working fast, and the elevator felt like it was spinning.

Forcing her eyes to focus, Marisol saw the number seven pop up in glowing red slashes on the floor display. Her limbs were getting heavy and she fought to keep her breathing shallow.

"Keep your eyes open." Marisol could hear the slur in her words and knew there wasn't much time left. "The minute the doors open, you run."

Marisol fell forward, but her shoulder hit hard into the metal wall. Sloane's body followed.

The display showed a five now, but it was swimming in front of her eyes.

"There's a police station three blocks to the east." Marisol's eyes crossed, so she could barely see the three pop up on the display. "Run out of the lobby and turn right. Don't stop for anything. Do you hear me?"

She told her arms to shake Sloane to make sure she was still conscious, but they didn't respond. She forced her gaze over her shoulder and there were trails in her vision. Sloane's eyes were closed and her neck limp. Marisol swore as the number two popped up.

It was the last thing she saw. Everything went black and she never felt her body hit the floor.

CHAPTER FOUR

Consciousness came and went for Sloane. Her eyelids were too heavy to lift and her ears felt clogged—like she was underwater. Her mind, normally so sharp and keen, couldn't make sense of anything.

Her eyes finally opened and she was hovering a foot off the ground, her blurry vision taking in pock-marked concrete, her nose full of gas station smells. Sound filtered into her ears and her mind catalogued it without making sense of the words.

…the Governor for fuck's sake…

I don't know what we're supposed to do with her either!

…wasn't supposed to be…

What happened to…

She must be dead.

But Sloane wasn't dead. Was she? This couldn't be what death felt like. Sharp pain in her ankles and shoulders. Harsh voices like no one she knew. The stink of oil and hot metal. Surely whatever afterlife existed had more to offer than this.

Sensation blinked out again as Sloane gave in to the weight pressing on her mind. It came back abruptly as her body hit the ground, but this ground was different. The sounds were different. Car horns and tires far away. She forced her eyes open. A face lay inches from her, making her flinch.

Marisol Soltero. She lay near Sloane, her cheek pressed hard into the dark, pebbly ground. Ever since Sloane had entered the prosecutor's office, she'd known that she'd make enemies of criminals. It had never occurred to her the lengths some of them would go to get to her. Marisol had been the most dangerous of Sloane's many targets, but she had also been the only one to slip away. She was the very reason Sloane had abandoned the State's Attorney's office in favor of politics. She knew all the legal loopholes that required closing because Marisol had utilized them all.

Suddenly Marisol's face was even closer and this time it was ringed by stars poking through the forest of high-rise buildings. Floating above her. For a heartbeat Sloane's stomach flipped at the familiarity of it, then Marisol sneered, her lips moving with soundless words. Her hands reached for Sloane's neck. Whatever drug she'd used, it wasn't enough to keep Sloane from fighting back. Just as fingers wrapped around her throat, she lashed out, her balled fist smashing into Marisol's eye. Only it wasn't Marisol's eye. The face above her had changed—stubble dotted a much wider jaw.

The man rolled away and Sloane struggled to her feet, stumbling again when her world tilted sickeningly. Hands scrabbled at her shins but her heel connected with something soft that grunted. She fought the urge to close her eyes and forced her feet to move again, propelling her another step. Shouting from far away and close. The world leapt up too quickly and she was on her knees, pain shooting through her. She scrambled forward on hands and knees but something blocked her path.

Marisol's body. She was dead but there was no blood. Sloane pushed her palms into the concrete and she was nearly to her feet again when Marisol's hands reached up and grabbed her. No. Not Marisol's hands. Marisol was dead. But her body was moving and she was groaning. Different hands like steel bands wrapped around her chest.

Sloane's feet came off the ground but she didn't fall. Her mind started to swim and she heard screaming. Screaming so loud it hurt her ears.

Shut that bitch up or we'll get caught!

I'm trying...

The voice cut off and Sloane's arm fell limply at her side. She tried to lift her hands, to fight off Marisol's men, but she couldn't move again. Her eyelids started to droop.

There were sirens all around her. Flashes of light in all colors of the rainbow pricked at her eyelids. She tried to shout again but nothing happened. Her eyelids wouldn't open.

The sirens were replaced by voices, mumbling and cursing and she knew that certain syllables—ones she caught more often than others—combined to form her name. Her whole body swayed like she was on the deck of a boat on storm-tossed Lake Michigan. She felt a body beside her again. Marisol? Sloane had been so close to freedom. If only she could've taken a few more steps. The world blinked out again.

The voices were different when she was able to lift her eyelids again. The men she'd heard before and a woman. Marisol? No. Sloane knew her voice well. She'd heard it often enough. The tap on Marisol's office phone had provided hours of mundane conversation concerning imports and exports. Calls she had known were code for something, but Sloane never found evidence that could convict.

What the fuck is this? My instructions were clear...

The cops were there too fast. Look, nothing happened like you said it would.

We did the best we could.

And you're coming with me so you can explain to the boss why...

She knew she'd recognize the sounds around her if only she could think.

...kill her and dump her

There's no time, you idiot. We have to get in the air. We're late as it is and the ground crew is already suspicious.

Sloane could only blink and take in the senseless words.

...put a bullet in her head and leave her here.

Great idea. I'm sure no one will care when the Governor of Illinois' body is found in the boss's private hangar. Cargo planes with no passengers drop off corpses all the time.

Those words registered and they set Sloane's limbs in motion. She tried to push herself to her feet. Marisol's people were going to kill her. Struggling for what felt like hours, she blinked and realized she hadn't moved a muscle. Even the blink had been a hard-won battle.

Just put her in the plane. Let the boss decide what to do.

A smear of dark moved in front of Sloane's line of sight. She blinked to clear the image, but her eyelids didn't reopen. After a moment she forgot that she'd been trying to open them. After another moment she was asleep again, this time so deeply she wouldn't move or think or remember.

CHAPTER FIVE

1985

Marisol tried to play with her bunny, but no matter how she hummed their little song or danced Bunny around on his dingy, tattered feet, she could still hear them yelling. She sat cross-legged on the living room floor, bouncing up and down on the carpet, humming for all her life. They were in the kitchen, yelling across the table. Well, Mommy wasn't yelling, she was pleading, begging and crying for him to stop yelling. He was yelling, but he was always yelling. Yelling and drinking from the fat square bottle that smelled icky.

She thought he was probably her daddy. She couldn't remember if he'd always been around, like Mommy had, or if he was new. It seemed like he was new, but Marisol wasn't sure. He'd been around as long as she'd had Bunny because Marisol remembered Bunny was new when she wanted to know what was in the square bottle and the man threw Bunny out the window and Marisol cried all night. Somehow she found him in the morning, but he'd been in the dirt by the dumpster and it had rained all night and Bunny wasn't new anymore after that.

Just then Mommy yelled really loud and Marisol looked up. The man that might have been her daddy had his hands around Mommy's neck and she was making a funny noise. Mommy put her hands up to his and her hands looked so little on his massive ones. Marisol covered Bunny's beady, plastic eyes with her hand until Mommy's foot stopped tapping against the open refrigerator door, but she kept her eyes wide open. She couldn't stop staring at how big his hands were.

Then Mommy was on the floor, looking across the tile at Marisol but something was wrong. She wasn't exactly looking at Marisol. She was looking above her, around her, through her. She was looking at everything. She was looking at nothing. Marisol held out her ratty little stuffed rabbit to Mommy, but she wouldn't take it.

The man that might have been her daddy sat down at the table and pulled the top off the square bottle. He tipped it to the ceiling, the brown liquid gurgled and sloshed around then all went away. He set the bottle down on the table. After another minute, he looked at Marisol.

That's when she got up and ran. Her feet were all full of pins and needles from sitting on the floor so long, but she ran anyway. She didn't know why at first, but it felt like the right idea to run, so she did. She ran right out the front door and onto the street. She hid from all the grown-up strangers and their questions when they saw her alone with Bunny. She hid from the older kids after they took Bunny, ripped off his ears and set him on fire, laughing as she cried.

No one came looking for her. No one knew she existed.

CHAPTER SIX

Marisol Soltero was a predator and, like any hunter, she awoke fully aware. Her eyes came into focus and she registered unfamiliar surroundings. Marisol never woke in a strange place. She needed to move, to back into a corner and gain a defensible position, but when she tried the hollow scraping of metal on metal burst in her ears. Jerking her limbs, a sharp pain cut into her wrists and ankles.

She was seated in a metal chair, her hands and feet shackled to it, a strap around her chest pulled so tightly she struggled to take a full breath. The room around her hummed with the throbbing, whining sound of a high-performance engine. The strange weightlessness that came with unexpected movement took over her body. Her mind was still sloshy from the dart and she shook her head to clear it.

Through the dim light of a flickering bulb overhead she saw a bank of seats, which might explain their stuttering movement. Her focus was drawn to the body draped across it. Governor Sloane lay unmoving across the worn surface, her dress streaked with dirt and an oily smear near her small, bare feet.

Marisol studied her, willing her chest to move and reveling in the chance to look at her up close for the first time in so many years. Sloane was a small woman, at least six inches shorter than Marisol, though her demeanor made her substantial. She still had the look of one who didn't have time to work out and didn't much care. She carried a few extra pounds but showed confidence in her own skin and both the weight and assurance looked good on her. Her long, waving hair was dark auburn. Her form-fitting dress accentuated her soft, feminine curves and the devastating shade of royal blue set off her fiery hair.

Her pearl solitaire necklace and diamond earrings were still in place, as were her tennis bracelet and rings. Marisol catalogued the information as the floor beneath her bumped and rattled. Letting Sloane keep her jewelry could be a sign that they were going to ransom her. If their kidnappers had removed them it was likely they'd already planned to kill her. Her hands were bound, but the ties were loose—far looser than Marisol's. Clearly they didn't see her as a threat and Marisol needed to ensure they continued to think that way.

No threat. Loosely bound. Jewelry in place. Why was Sloane here? They'd tried to kill her and failed, but brought her along anyway. Marisol had worked with enough unimaginative underlings to guess. The elevator had opened on the lobby to show two unconscious women and none of their cohorts. They had to know the police were on the way. Without the time to go upstairs and figure out what happened, they would have to make a split-second decision. So they'd decided to not make a decision at all. They'd brought Sloane to their bosses to make the final call. The reprieve was just fine with Marisol. She could exploit it.

Sloane began to waken, groaning and struggling to push herself up. At the same time the low, whining rumble all around her increased in volume. Marisol was thrown back against her seat and the realization hit her so hard she spoke the words aloud.

"An airplane."

She felt the moment the landing gear left the tarmac, the weightlessness of flying momentarily overwhelming her.

Reality crashed down at the knowledge they were being taken out of the city, most likely out of the state. It was a risky move, transporting kidnapped individuals across state lines, but they had already proven themselves competent, incapacitating the Queen of Humboldt and separating the Governor of Illinois from her layers of protection.

When the plane banked, the pull of gravity sent a sharp stab of pain through her temple. She saw a similar wince from Sloane. What had they used to knock them out? Marisol pondered possible long-term effects to distract herself from the pain blossoming across her forehead. The higher they climbed, the more acute the throbbing until she had to grit her teeth against it. Sloane let out a weak cry of pain, pressing her bound palms against her brow and finally sitting up. The plane finished its turn and settled into a straight climb. The pain lessened when the plane leveled out, just a ghost of discomfort lingering as they cruised along.

Marisol scanned the cabin—she thought she'd heard a noise behind her, but the roar of the engines was too loud to be sure. The bonds holding Marisol to her chair limited her movement. Chains rattled on hollow metal as she tested the limits, but they held fast. Sloane raised her head and looked around, drawing Marisol's complete attention. Sloane's eyes landed on her. Marisol smirked and prepared a snide greeting when her eyes bulged with fear.

"Marisol!"

It was probably meant to be a scream, but it came out as a sleepy croak. At the same moment Marisol caught a flash of movement in her peripheral vision. A fist exploded into her jaw and she was unconscious before her chin landed on her chest.

CHAPTER SEVEN

1992

Rain poured down in icy sheets. The park's paved pathways rippled with little waves of water like the surface of the nearby river. Even under the cover of the bridge, droplets found their way to Marisol's skin. They bounced up to soak the fabric of her too-short jeans. They found the cracks in the soles of her Converse High Tops. They hung, quivering and delicate, on the frayed edge of her baseball cap before plopping down onto the knees she hugged to her chest.

Two nights ago Marisol had lost her jacket in a fight with some older kids, so her flannel button-up was soaked through. She made sure her body didn't shiver, though. No one would know she was cold and miserable in the autumn thunderstorm. No one would know the thunderclaps made her jump because she only jumped inside. Outside she was tough. Outside, she was no one to be messed with.

"Hey."

Marisol ignored the voice at first. She always ignored adult voices.

"Hey! Marisol!"

She recognized the voice at the sound of her name. Looking up, she saw the only face that smiled when it looked at her.

"Hey, Ruby."

"What're you doing under there, kid?" Ruby shifted the cheap plastic umbrella in her hand and stuck her head farther under the bridge, out of the storm's noise. "Didn't I tell you to come to me when you needed help?"

"Don't need help."

"Course ya don't." Ruby laughed as she held out her free hand. "Come on, get your ass movin'."

Marisol smiled and took Ruby's hand. It was warm and soft and wrapped around Marisol's shoulder while they walked together under the umbrella.

Ruby was a hooker. They'd met a year ago when Marisol had tried to pick a guy's pocket outside Tiger Stadium. The guy had nearly broken her wrist when he grabbed her, but Ruby had stepped in, distracting him with her halter top while Marisol had made a run for it. Tracking her down outside a popular burger place, Ruby had paid for lunch.

She had won Marisol's trust by not asking where her parents were or why she was living on the street. Ruby had sipped her soda through a straw covered in bright red lipstick and told funny stories about the stray cat living on her fire escape. After that, Marisol had spent a couple days a week hanging out with Ruby. On game days they would work together, Ruby distracting drunk idiots while Marisol lifted their wallets.

Ruby was the most beautiful woman she'd ever seen. She teased her white-blond hair up into a mass of feather-light curls and her skin was soft as a new T-shirt. Marisol was old enough to realize she'd had a puppy-dog crush on Ruby early on, but now she felt more like a big sister. And she'd helped Marisol get really good at picking pockets. Not good enough to have a steady place to stay when the weather was crappy, but Ruby always tracked her down and brought her in out of the rain.

Times were tough for Ruby at the moment, too. The cops in her old neighborhood had started cracking down on the working girls so she'd moved closer to downtown. Her new place was a room in a rickety old motel she rented by the week, but she said it was safer. She even had a few regulars who had her address and fixed appointments.

Marisol and Ruby stopped for the new Crystal Pepsi that Ruby loved so much and hot dogs to take back to the room. Marisol could barely keep the saliva in her mouth. Nothing had been going her way recently and she hadn't eaten in a few days. All her cash had been in the pocket of the Detroit Tigers jacket she'd lost. Ruby kept telling her it'd be easier if she stopped fighting with the other kids and made a few friends, but it was a tough sell to ask Marisol to like anyone.

"Why don't you shower before dinner? You smell like a drowned rat." Ruby tossed her key on the flimsy table in the corner. She turned her thousand-watt smile on Marisol, yanking the dirty cap off her head. "You kinda look like one, too, kid. I dig the haircut though."

Marisol blushed and rubbed a hand through the uneven chunks of her hair. She'd cut it herself yesterday at a day shelter she went to sometimes. The bathroom mirror had been cloudy and small, and it was hard to get to the back of her head, but she'd done the best she could and liked having her hair short. It felt better than the tight ponytail she'd always worn.

"Thanks."

Ruby reached out and ruffled Marisol's hair, the wet, greasy strands flopped against Marisol's burning cheeks. "Want me to clean it up a little later?"

"Sure."

"Tell ya what," Ruby said, bending to look into Marisol's eyes. "Why don't we eat first? You can shower after. I'm starved."

Marisol shrugged like she didn't care, but her stomach growled at the same moment, ruining the effect. Ruby didn't say anything, just hung up her coat in the closet with the flimsy accordion doors. They ate and chatted while they watched TV. After *Full House* ended, Marisol took a shower using Ruby's shampoo-conditioner combination. Ruby hung out in the bathroom with her, choosing to continue their conversation because neither of them liked *Hangin' with Mr. Cooper*. Ruby wrapped the still-damp towel around Marisol's shoulders and tidied up her hair during *Roseanne*.

Coach was just starting when there was a knock at the door.

"Shoot," Ruby said, jumping up and looking at her watch. "Marisol, darlin', can you…"

"Sure, Ruby. I know the drill."

Marisol turned off the TV on her way to the closet. She had a blanket in there and a pillow. Stuffed underneath them inside an old shoebox were her battered Walkman and a few cassettes. The foam was worn away on one side of the headphones, so the metal speaker bit into her ear, but they were loud enough to block out the sound of Ruby working. Marisol didn't have time to pick a new cassette. She had barely pulled the blanket over her body just in case the john peeked in the closet, when she heard a muffled male voice. She pushed play just in time to cover Ruby's giggling.

The Red Hot Chili Peppers started singing about a bridge downtown and Marisol let Flea's bass lines take her away and escape life for a bit. Escape the memories of her mother's empty eyes. Escape the loneliness and the isolation. Always wanting what she couldn't have. Always hungry and cold. The beatings from the gang girls. The insults from the guys who'd called her a "lez" when she'd cut her hair.

When something slammed into the door, Marisol thought she'd gotten carried away again, banging her head to the music. She had to be quiet and still. Then it happened again, this time she was sure the impact was from the outside. It bent the door off its track and a crack of light came into the closet. Marisol was trying to shimmy back into the shadows when she heard the sharp impact of skin on skin and Ruby's whimper. Marisol didn't know much, but she knew what it sounded like when a man slapped a woman's face.

Marisol leaned forward to see through the slit just in time to watch the john toss Ruby across the room. She landed on the bed and tried to scramble to her feet, but he was on her in a flash. His hands wrapped around her neck as she scratched at his arms, leaving little red streaks as her face turned red and then purple.

Marisol tried to stand. She tried to shout. She tried to rush out of the closet and attack the man. She couldn't move. Her limbs were frozen in place. All she could do was watch Ruby's face turn darker purple and her fingers stop scratching. He let her go and stood up. He swore and kicked at her foot. Ruby's shoe fell off, but she didn't move.

The guy straightened his clothes, grabbed his jacket and left. Marisol sat staring at Ruby's bare foot through "My Lovely Man" and "Sir Psycho Sexy". She'd played the cassette so often that the tape was stretched at the end. The cover of "They're Red Hot" played with a slow, distorted voice that would have been creepy in someone else's life.

The tape finished and the Walkman snapped to a stop, the play button popping back up and making Marisol jump. She dropped it and the force ripped the headphones off her ears. When she stood up, Ruby's clothes brushed against her body, surrounding her in the smell of cheap perfume, cheaper cologne and unwashed fabric. They smelled like Ruby.

Marisol pushed out of the closet and slid under the bed. She pried up the loose floorboard and grabbed the wad of cash Ruby kept in an old cigar box. There was a battered photograph of a couple wearing clothes from the seventies and a kid who had Ruby's perfect smile and crooked nose. Marisol left the photo but took the gold watch and diamond earrings. She slid out the other side of the bed to keep her back to Ruby's body.

She didn't look back at the bed. She grabbed her cap and the bag of corn chips from the table and slipped out the door, back into a world that wouldn't let her keep anyone she loved.

CHAPTER EIGHT

The pain in Marisol's jaw jogged her awake. She hadn't woken up to a sore jaw in so long, it made her feel twenty years old and seventy years old simultaneously. Back when she was a lowly grunt, skipping all over town with no map and no compass, moral or otherwise, living off what her fists and guns could bring her, it was pretty much how every morning started. Back before she had legitimate businesses to run that required a boss without a bruised face. It was astonishing how much time a business front took to maintain.

She listened hard for any sounds around her, but the roar of jet engines was too loud. Snapping her eyes open, she searched for Sloane. Before she could do a sweep of the cramped cabin, her eyes settled on a woman leaning against the far wall. She wore a smug, irritating smile and, as she always did when she saw that grin, Marisol longed to wipe it off her face.

"Jordan. What's a shriveled up *coño* like you doing in a nice place like this?"

The smug smile wavered slightly on Jordan's lips. Resentment curled its edges, but she managed to make it stick. "Happy to see me, Marisol?"

"Thrilled," she replied sarcastically.

Jordan was so set on appearing relaxed that her entire body was rigid. It didn't fit well on her frame, like a too-big glove in danger of falling off. It had been several years since Marisol had seen her. She would be thirty by now, a decade younger than Marisol and unremarkable in every way. Average height, average build, short mousey-brown hair and regular features. Jordan had signed on to Marisol's outfit early and expected to be rewarded well for it, but she lacked the imagination to be useful. Marisol had hooked up with her a few times out of boredom, then discovered the one thing she didn't lack was ambition.

That ambition would have been something to monitor if Marisol had been a simple criminal. Because her circumstances were more complex, it had seemed prudent to get Jordan's ambition as far away as possible. Marisol had shipped her off to help operations in a backwater town and promptly forgot about her. Apparently that had been a mistake.

"It's been a long time, Marisol."

There was just as much tension in Jordan's voice as her posture. There had always been a shadow of awe in the way Jordan had looked at Marisol, even when they were intimate, and she couldn't hide the fact that it was still there.

"Not long enough," she answered. "Been keeping busy since we last met?"

Jordan looked around the cabin. "Very busy. Though I regret to inform you that I have to resign my position with your outfit."

"A great loss to the business, I'm sure. Though, if I recall, you weren't making me a lot of money. The team in Joliet made twice as much as you last year."

"Fuck the team from Joliet and fuck Peoria. I can't believe you shipped me out there."

"You could've done well in Peoria, but you obviously had other deals distracting you."

"You're goddamn right I did."

Marisol had always been good at reading people. It was why she had been so successful. She could tell what they were thinking and could use it against them. When she glanced across the room, she saw how the evening's events were taking a toll on Sloane. She sat too straight, looking purposefully at nothing. After a heartbeat, she glanced at Marisol, giving her the same look of mild distaste Marisol remembered so well from their previous meetings, but there was something else there, too. An undercurrent of desperation. Her nerves were stretched thin and she wouldn't be able to handle too much of this. Marisol tucked that away for later.

"Well, you've certainly come up in the world. Tell me, Jordan, did you come up by going down?"

She grinned into the insult, taking the moment while Jordan seethed to look around the room. They weren't in the plane's passenger cabin. The walls and floor were bare metal with nothing to muffle the roaring engines. Boxes strapped with netting to the walls on either side suggested a cargo hold. The short wall in front of her held a metal door secured by a formidable bar lock and the seats where Sloane sat with her prim, perfect posture that were so odd in the circumstance.

Marisol was in the center of the open space. Tapping her boot against the chair leg, she heard the echo of hollow metal and felt the thick bolt locking the chair to the floor. Nylon rope bound her legs and chest to the chair while simple metal handcuffs restrained her hands behind her. If she could move a leg, she could bend the legs or smash the welds but she didn't have the leverage to scratch her ankle, much less break free.

Jordan's eyes tracked her movements. "Not the throne you're used to as the Queen of Humboldt." She sneered out the title, her anger making Marisol's chest swell with pride. "But it'll have to do."

"You afraid of me, Jordan?"

"I know you. That's why I strapped you down like a rabid dog."

"I seem to recall you liked it better when I tied you up."

A blush crept across Jordan's cheeks. "You don't know me like you used to."

"I can barely remember. You didn't leave much of an impression."

Jordan's face grew redder, from anger this time.

Sloane squirmed in her seat. "Whoever you are, I demand…"

Marisol shot her a warning look, but Jordan shouted her response first.

"Shut up, Governor." Her head snapped around to face Sloane, her eyes wild. "I've been extremely polite to you so far, but that can change at any moment."

Sloane went quiet, but she didn't look half as frightened as she should've been. Jordan had been famous for her volatile temper. It was the reason no one in the gang was too sad to see her banished to suburban hell. Maybe Sloane had a temper herself—she looked like she wanted to shout back. Warning bells sounded in Marisol's head.

"Why have you been so kind to Governor Sloane? You did try to kill her. In fact, Plan B was far more effective than Plan A. Why the crude initial attempt?"

The acknowledgement of her success wasn't exactly a compliment, but it was soothing enough to turn her attention back to Marisol, who allowed herself a single, shallow breath.

"It would only be crude if my goal was to kill her."

"What was the goal then? If you were trying to tickle the Governor, you've taken an odd approach."

"Oh no, not yet." Jordan waved her finger in the air. "This goes at my pace."

"You shouldn't be able to afford a plane like this, Jordan. You shouldn't be able to afford a plane at all on what I pay you."

She strode across the cabin, sliding her fingertips across Marisol's back as she circled behind her.

"You aren't the only one who pays me." She stood in front of Marisol, crowding her space. "I've been two-timing for a while now. That's something you should know all about."

Shock boiled up inside Marisol but she forced her features to remain neutral. All these years and no one had figured out her secret. She'd been careful—so damn careful. How could an idiot like Jordan figure it out?

She flicked her eyes to Sloane, who was staring with disgust at the back of Jordan's head. Her chest was heaving and her frayed edges were becoming more evident. Time was up. Marisol needed time to think and Sloane needed the room empty.

Marisol swallowed hard and let her eyes drift languorously up Jordan's body. She put a seductive purr in her voice and was pleased to hear Jordan's breath hitch as she spoke, "But darling, two-timing? You shouldn't even be able to sell that." She shot a grin at Jordan's crotch. "You're shit in bed, *cariño*. You'd be lucky to be able to give it away. Unless you've learned some new tricks in the last few years. Or, you know, any tricks at all."

The first punch landed on Marisol's left flank and pushed every ounce of air out of her. The second landed on her right and the world tilted on its axis. She smiled and a fist smashed into her nose, taking her off into oblivion.

CHAPTER NINE

1996

The boombox was playing so loudly the whole thing vibrated, rattling against the heavy oak tabletop. Three men in identical grey suits leaned over it, rocking to the frenetic beat. Each had the telltale bulge of a handgun at their armpit, straining the cheap fabric. None of them paid any attention to the door, even when it opened.

Marisol slipped in quietly, letting the music cover her entrance. The song was from the new Beastie Boys album. She didn't know the name of the track, but she recognized it from her many trips to lift CDs from the store. That album sold well on the street.

Her gang followed her into the warehouse. Only five of them were willing to risk Marisol's plan, and four of the five looked like they regretted their bravado already. Only Gray looked confident. He had her back, and that was all she needed. The rest of them were just a show of force. All they had to do was wait until after the deal was done to piss their pants.

She stepped into the light and crossed her arms, her gang

spreading out behind her. It took several long moments before the idiots listening to their hip hop noticed the intruders. Marisol focused her attention on the obvious leader, a man with slicked-back hair and Ray-Bans. He leaped to his feet when he spotted her, slapping the nearest lackey, who switched off the boombox.

"What's this?" Ray-Ban asked, an oily grin splitting his lips. "The Girl Scouts sellin' cookies?"

His accent had a cadence familiar from New York cop shows and a fake tan turned his pale skin orange.

"I believe you were expecting us," Marisol said, keeping her arms folded.

The men laughed, deeply and in unison. Marisol felt her face go hot, which only made them laugh louder. Finally, Ray-Ban held up his hand and the room went silent.

"You're in the wrong room, little girl. Walk away and I'll forget I saw you here." He paused for a moment before saying in a less friendly tone, "This is the only chance I'll give you."

The laughter chafed but it didn't deter Marisol. She held out her hand to Gray and he handed her a bulging duffel bag. The weight of it pulled her shoulder uncomfortably, but she never broke eye contact with Ray-Ban while she unzipped it and dropped it onto the floor at her feet. Gold watches and glittering diamonds spilled out onto the dusty concrete and the men stopped laughing.

Ray-Ban sucked his teeth, then snapped his fingers, sending a minion scurrying from the room. The leader cut an impressive figure, waiting with meaty arms folded across his chest. Well over six feet tall with a neck the size of a tree trunk and hands like sledgehammers, he would intimidate any sixteen-year-old girl, even one with something to prove. Marisol, who wasn't just any sixteen-year-old girl and had nothing to prove, was not intimidated.

The guy returned, pushing a rolling cart out of the shadows into the light by the table. It was piled high with strapped bundles of cash—twenties and fifties and a few smaller packs of hundreds. Marisol felt the girl to her right stiffen and twitch at the sight. She could almost hear her entire crew salivating at the sight of so much money.

"One hundred k, as agreed." Ray-Ban strode across the room, waving his arm like some after-school special version of Vanna White to indicate his payment. "That's if the goods are genuine."

"They're genuine," Marisol replied, watching him closely.

Ray-Ban bent to lift a diamond necklace from the floor, fitting a jeweler's glass to his eye. While he inspected the necklace one of his men turned out the bag on the table, the tangle of chains, rings and watches glittering in the low light.

"You raid ya momma's jewelry box for this stuff?" Ray-Ban asked, tossing the necklace onto the table with the rest of the loot.

"You don't need to know how we got it," Marisol replied, sticking her chin out as far as she could manage. "I charge extra for story time."

"Don't be an idiot!" he shouted, making everyone jump except Marisol and Gray. "There's no place for you in this. This is a game for adults. No kids allowed."

It was time, and Marisol was ready. She yanked the Glock from her waistband. It was absurdly large in her hands, but the weight was familiar as she leveled it at Ray-Ban's chest. His goons weren't quick enough, and she had him in her sights before they could raise their weapons. Gray and the rest of Marisol's gang belatedly whipped out their own guns.

"I have the product and you have the network to move what I've got. There are two choices. You can buy from me and we can all make a killing." Her heart pounded, thrilled at the standoff she'd created. "Or I can make a killing now and keep it all for myself."

Ray-Ban laughed. It echoed maniacally in the silent warehouse, bouncing off the cocked guns and reverberating in the nervous sweat on everyone's forehead. He started a slow, sinister clap that echoed his slow, sinister march right into Marisol's space. She held him with her eyes, waiting for his next move. He got into her face, his breath reeking of garlic.

"I like you, little girl." He reached for her face and she pushed the barrel of her Glock against his chest. He paused for a moment, but when she didn't fire, he ran thick fingers through her short, choppy hair. "You're like me. Except one thing."

"What's that?"

The smile vanished from his face, replaced by a snarl. His hand went from her hair to her neck in a flash, the pad of his thumb pressing against her throat. Before she could register her breath being cut off, he pulled out a flashy, chrome-plated Colt 45.

"I've got a bigger…"

He never finished the sentence. Marisol squeezed the trigger and he jerked back from her. She squeezed the trigger again and he released her neck. She squeezed it a third time and smelled burning fabric.

There was a heartbeat of pure, unadulterated silence. Marisol breathed into it, filled it with her oxygen and her spirit. She stared into Ray-Ban's eyes while the light went out of them. Gravity took over and he tipped backward, slamming into the concrete floor.

As Marisol exhaled, the world split apart. With a flick of her wrist she flipped the table. The jewelry her gang had collected through months of picking pockets, breaking into houses and knocking over one poorly secured pawn shop skittered across the floor, sending up sparkles of refracted light. Thunder erupted from a thousand places and she ducked behind the table. The surface jerked and shook as bullet after bullet slammed into it. Marisol took two deep breaths then glided out to her right. She popped off two shots in quick succession, then shifted her angle and fired another pair. She was back behind the table when she heard a body hit the floor.

Splintering screeches accompanied her next three breaths. The table was buckling under the shower of bullets. She needed to move faster. Marisol gritted her teeth and popped out of cover again. She squeezed twin shots at her target, but they went wide. She felt the wind of a bullet pass close to her left cheek, but ducked behind the splintering table in time to take the last few seconds of safety it could provide. She smelled the warm, sweet scent of sawdust as each new bullet lodged into the thick tabletop. There was only one guy left and Marisol knew she would win. She fired off two more shots before her clip went dry.

She dropped the Glock and rolled over her left shoulder to where Ray-Ban's pistol had fallen. She scooped it up, enjoying its weight in her hand for a split second before using it to blast out a grey suit-clad kneecap. With a howl of pain he fell and she sent the next round into the crown of his head, plunging the warehouse into echoing silence.

Surveying the room, Marisol saw bodies down on both sides. To her immense surprise, she noted that her people weren't injured, only cowering in fear. Gray was the only one on his feet and his face was pale as death, the gun in his hand shook dangerously. Gray had shown well during the fight and proven himself to Marisol.

Marisol felt no fear or shock at the scene around her. This was exactly how she'd imagined it playing out. The best possible result, she thought as Gray collected the scattered jewelry. She turned the Colt over in her hands, the chrome flashing in her eye. She had certainly come out on top today.

CHAPTER TEN

The sight of blood dripping from Marisol's nose onto her leather pants in a slow, monotonous rhythm set Sloane's teeth on edge. She had not led a quiet life since her gubernatorial victory. Aides, secretaries, lobbyists and other politicians constantly surrounded her. Her phone buzzed with emails and text messages at all hours. Being alone in this small space with an unconscious, bleeding companion was unsettling. She tried to clear her mind how her yoga instructor advised, but it was impossible. She had to stop the blood plunking on stretched leather or she would scream.

She couldn't understand why it was taking so long for Marisol to wake. The beating was terrifyingly extensive, but Jordan had left with bloody knuckles and a wide smile ages ago. As little experience as Sloane had with this sort of violence, she still felt that Marisol should be conscious by now. She let out an exasperated breath and fidgeted, looking over at Marisol for the hundredth time just to be sure she was still breathing.

The rope stretched across Marisol's chest kept her upright and Sloane studied her profile. Her chiseled jaw was an angry red on the left side. Her nose was split along the bridge, oozing dark red blood, but it still maintained the straight, graceful slope that had first caught Sloane's eye. She stared at it long enough to see a bead rise from the flesh. Soon it would grow too heavy to maintain its precarious position and it would fall onto Marisol's pants, pressing Sloane a little closer to the edge of sanity.

"Are you awake?" She tested her voice, trying to be heard over the dull roar of the plane, but it came out quiet and croaky. "Marisol?"

No response. Not surprising from such a worthless creature.

Sloane had just passed her bar exams when Marisol had dropped into Chicago out of nowhere. She'd made a name for herself quickly and, apparently Sloane had been the only one who'd never heard of their new criminal hot shot. That oversight wouldn't be repeated and she made sure, from that day at the courthouse forward, that no one so much as stole a candy bar in her town without her knowing about it. Over the next six years, Sloane had earned her reputation taking down Chicago's rankest scum as well as a few crooked politicians, and then won the election for State's Attorney by a landslide. She'd thought by the time Marisol's name came up in connection with one of her first SA cases she could conduct the deposition herself rather than passing it off to a junior lawyer. She had realized her mistake the moment she'd laid eyes on Marisol again.

Sloane prided herself on her good taste. She loved fine art, with a penchant for the Pre-Raphaelites. She loved violin music and well-tailored clothes. She appreciated beauty in all its forms, and she would not apologize for that. So it was unfortunate how distractingly beautiful Marisol Soltero was. Her confident smile that would make any woman swoon. It was unfortunate and infuriating. Marisol was a liar. A criminal. A modern-day pirate with the insufferable arrogance to style herself The Queen of Humboldt. She was everything that Sloane detested.

Had Marisol been a law-abiding citizen—a teacher or a doctor, hell, even if she waited tables at some dive café—Sloane would defy her critics and friends alike and throw herself at her without shame or regret. But god had a sick sense of humor. The angel's face was attached to a devil's body.

Sloane could not abide a lawbreaker, no matter how much they made her mouth water and her mind wander. She had spent every moment of her adult life trying to make the world a better place. As Governor, she pursued peace and cooperation bound by the clear lines of fair and just laws. Marisol lived outside those lines.

Now that she could admire Marisol at close, albeit horrendous quarters again, some of the mystique was wearing off. Marisol's bravery was admirable, but it was completely pointless. She needled Jordan purposefully, increasing her punishment. And for what? No doubt the result would serve Marisol and no one else. The Queen of Humboldt indeed.

The people of Humboldt Park were not the poorest in the city, but the community was majority Puerto Rican and they faced insidious discrimination. The L bypassed Humboldt and the bus system was only marginally more available. Most of the neighborhood qualified as a food desert. With no grocery stores willing to invest in the area, a trip for food was a day-long event. With Marisol's violent gang in charge, that situation was unlikely to change. What Humboldt needed was protection from the law, not from a gang leader.

Anger flared in Sloane and it pushed her to her feet. She took a few, halting steps across the cabin. With her shackled hands Sloane awkwardly yanked a paisley bandana hanging out of Marisol's pants pocket. Taking a deep breath, she knelt in front of her, listening closely to see she had woken her, but her breathing was just as even as before.

The tight fabric of Sloane's dress pinched around her knees as she knelt. She was second-guessing her decision to approach her fellow prisoner. Being this close, smelling Marisol's fresh blood and sweat, reminded Sloane viscerally of who this woman was.

The thought of her victims was in the forefront of Sloane's mind as she dabbed the bandana against Marisol's bleeding nose. She'd meant to be gentle, but Marisol's flinch told Sloane it had hurt. She scooted away involuntarily, prepared to defend herself.

Sloane summoned her resolve. She was being ridiculous. She was no wilting flower. Marisol was bound. She was not a threat. Moreover, Sloane was a woman of action. This cowering did not become her. She stiffened her spine and felt better than she had since the first gunshot this evening.

This time she pressed the fabric firmly against Marisol's nose, pinching the bridge to stop the bleeding. Marisol grunted and stirred. One simultaneous, sharp movement from both of them caused a wet, crunching sound from Marisol's nose. Sloane winced, waiting for the roar of pain and anger, but none came. Marisol's eyes opened and fixed on her. Sloane held them for a moment, then looked pointedly away.

When the bleeding had stopped, Sloane pulled the bandana away, leaving a sticky trail along the bridge of her nose. She wiped it again and Marisol hissed in pain.

"That hurts, you know."

"Yes, well, I suppose you're familiar with being bloodied up."

Marisol grinned. Her teeth were stained with blood. "It is an occupational hazard."

Sloane dabbed at her lip impatiently. "Did you have to be so disagreeable?"

Marisol's voice was low and rough. "It's in my nature, dear."

The familiarity made Sloane's cheeks burn. "Perhaps you should embrace a better nature. I'm sure we wouldn't be in this predicament if you weren't such a hedonistic, lawless, selfish criminal."

"On the contrary, Governor." Jordan's voice boomed out with shocking malice from behind Sloane. "If that was all Marisol was, I would have no use for her at all. Sit back down."

Sloane had her eyes on Marisol, her concern rising to the surface with surprising speed. The first two times Jordan had come in, she'd knocked Marisol unconscious. Her return did not bode well—even if Sloane wasn't exactly sympathetic, she did not like to see anyone hurt. Marisol gave her the ghost of a wink and motioned her chin toward the chairs across the room. Somehow, even though Marisol must know nothing good was likely to happen with Jordan back, she seemed confident and that bolstered Sloane's resolve. She stood with dignity, but she did not return to her seat as instructed.

"I demand an explanation."

"You demand, do you?"

"Yes. I do. I want to know why you killed my security detail and why you tried to kill me. I want to know why you kidnapped me. What do you want?"

"I want you to sit back down."

"I'm not afraid of you."

Jordan's eyes flashed as she bolted forward, forcing Sloane back until she was pressed against a cargo net.

"You should be."

Her eyes crawled over Sloane. A buzz of fear filled Sloane's ears and she felt the blood drain from her face. The moment Jordan stepped back, she slipped across the cabin and sat down.

"I believe," Marisol said, drawing Jordan's attention away. Sloane felt the moment those eyes left her, allowing her lungs to expand. "You were going to tell me why you weren't trying to kill Governor Sloane."

"Was I?"

Jordan was warming to her task. Whether it was the obvious success she had intimidating Sloane or the sight of Marisol's bruised face, she seemed more confident.

"I suppose now's as good a time as any." She paced while she lectured. "Governor Sloane was not the target. Had you arrived on the scene later, she would be dead and that would've been fine. You were the real target."

"Me?"

"You are far more valuable than our Governor."

Marisol cut her eyes across at Sloane for a heartbeat. There was an unreadable look in those regal features, but, in the space of a breath, she returned her focus to her tormentor.

"Then why go after her at all?"

"Because I know the best way to lure you away from your den," Jordan swept the room with a smile directed at Sloane. "Is to threaten her."

The words landed in Sloane's brain like a physical blow, knocking her off center. The statement made no sense to her. Apart from the irrational pleasure Marisol had always taken in provoking Sloane, there was no obvious reason that she would think about her at all, much less care if someone threatened her.

"Twitchy D," Marisol whispered, shaking her head.

"He'll do anything for a fix, *Your Majesty*." She added a simpering, pathetic tone to the title. "Tweakers are so easy to manipulate. I just fed him the info and complained that you wouldn't trust a warning from me. He practically begged for permission to pass it along."

"You used him."

Jordan leaned over and swept a stubby finger across Marisol's jaw. "I learned from the best."

Sloane's confusion morphed into withering disdain. They'd been lovers, that much had been obvious from the start, but now Sloane could see how much they deserved each other.

"If this is about blackmail, I wrote the book. Don't challenge a master," Marisol said.

"I think you know what this is about."

"We tried that once before, Jordan. I recall being unsatisfied by the encounter, but you did…give it your all. Maybe if you've learned your way around a bedroom in the last few years, I'll give you a chance to make up for it."

With an open palm Jordan slapped her hard across the cheek. The sound made Sloane wince, as did the splotches that appeared on Marisol's face.

"That's more like it." Marisol flexed her thighs beneath her chains and smiled. Fresh blood shone on her teeth in the half-light of the cargo hold. "I want my lovers to show a little spirit."

Jordan reached up, her fingertips brushing over the imprint of her hand on Marisol's cheek. "I've missed this face." Her touch went to caress one thick, dark eyebrow and then the other. "I don't want to mar this face, Marisol. Please don't make me."

"Whether it's bleeding or whole," Marisol sneered. "It'll never be yours again."

Jordan's face was in front of hers in a flash, her teeth bared and a growl bubbling in the back of her throat. She shouted in a low, barely controlled voice, "Where is The Hotel?"

Sloane felt like she'd walked into the wrong room. The non sequitur caught her off guard, but she didn't have time to wonder about it.

"There are a lot of hotels in the world, Jordan. It depends on where you want to go."

Jordan slid onto Marisol's lap, straddling her in the chair. Marisol's groan of pain, the first she'd uttered all night, made Jordan laugh sickeningly.

"You know where I want to go?" She ran rough fingers over Marisol's face. "I want to go where I'm the queen and you're my slave. Where I have all the power and the beautiful women draped all over me every night. I want you on your knees, begging. That's where I want to go."

Marisol laughed. She threw her head back and opened her mouth wide and tossed wild shouts of glee at the ceiling. The sound was hollow even to Sloane's ears as she watched Jordan stiffen and stand.

"I'm afraid you can't afford the airfare on that one, *princesa*."

"I have my own plane, remember?"

As they swapped barbs, Sloane watched the exchange like a tennis match though she felt like she didn't know the rules.

"And we already established that's not enough to turn me on."

"It better be enough to get you talking," Jordan countered, her hands back on Marisol's face, pressing at her prominent cheekbones. "Or that little redhead who was grinding on you tonight will be crying alone."

"You know what that's like, don't you Jordan? Grinding on me and then spending the night crying alone?"

Jordan's false confidence snapped. Her probing fingers curled into a fist and smashed into Marisol's gut.

"Where's The Hotel?"

"I assume you want one that charges by the hour? Although, for you we can go with one that charges by the minute."

Her face contorted in rage and she raised her fist again. "Stop it!"

Sloane found herself on her feet as her own shout died away. Jordan's eyes, wild and bloodshot, turned on Sloane. Marisol's found her too, though her eyes held a note of warning.

"I want answers," Sloane said into the new quiet. "Nothing you're saying makes sense."

"It doesn't need to make sense to you," Jordan said, stalking toward her. "You aren't even supposed to be here. If it weren't for the idiots I work with, you'd be dead and Marisol and I would be sharing this lovely trip alone."

"That's the part that doesn't make sense!" Frustration had overridden her fear and she ignored the threat in favor of answers. "You said I was bait for her. That's preposterous."

"Isn't it?" Jordan was in her face again, bringing the reek of cologne applied so liberally it smelled like pure alcohol. "The question is: why?"

"Why what?"

"Why would she save you?"

Jordan's gaze roamed over Sloane's body, making her feel exposed. She didn't like the renewed interest.

"I think we both know it's not out of the goodness of her heart," Sloane sneered.

"Of course not." Marisol's voice was strained. "I don't have any."

"No dispute there," Jordan said, rubbing her chin as she continued her inspection. "But Marisol Soltero always has a reason. There's always something in it for her. What've you got on her?"

"If I had anything concrete she'd be in jail right now."

Jordan grinned as she circled Sloane, her words arriving on a breath against Sloane's shoulder. "Or wrapped around your little finger. Is she someone watching your back?"

The accusation wasn't completely off base. Sloane knew of at least one predecessor in the Governor's Mansion who had that very arrangement. That wasn't how her administration ran, however. "She might be corrupt slime, but I'm not."

"No, you aren't," Jordan said, slipping around Sloane so closely their bodies brushed. She tapped a fingernail to her teeth and said, "You're a Girl Scout if ever there was one."

"I don't like your tone."

Jordan ignored her words and her angry step forward. She turned her attention back to the chair bolted to the center of the floor. "Is that it, Marisol? Is she your handler?"

"Can't you just knock me out again? It'd be so much better than listening to you talk."

"What do you mean 'her handler'?" Sloane asked.

Yet another mysterious comment added to this infuriating conversation, and she was ready to scream. But Jordan was ignoring her again, her focus entirely on Marisol.

"Boss has known for a while that there's someone in Chicago pulling your strings." With a flurry of movement, Jordan was in Sloane's face again. "Is it you?"

Sloane held her ground. "I don't know what you're talking about."

A sly smile crept across Jordan's lips. "Of course you don't."

Movement behind Jordan made Sloane look over her shoulder. Marisol's face, which had been a mask of calm, had cracked into something close to fear. If Sloane had thought a black-hearted criminal could feel fear, she might've been concerned, but just as quickly as the look arrived, it disappeared.

Her eyes on Sloane, Jordan ran a hand through her hair and chuckled as she left the room without another word.

CHAPTER ELEVEN

The hatch slid shut with a loud clang. The lock mechanics creaked as they slammed into place. Marisol listened, trying to determine her chances of breaking through the door. It sounded far too solid, even if she could get out of the chair.

"What was she talking about?"

Marisol's torso was starting to hurt. She clenched her abs and a jolt of pain throbbed through her. Trying to flex rapidly cramping muscles was an orchestra of aches, but she knew her body would feel much worse before this ordeal was over.

"Why did she think I was your handler? Why would you have a handler?"

Ignoring the volley of questions from Sloane was easy. Ignoring those rocketing around her mind was much harder. How did Jordan of all people know about The Hotel? Marisol had spent every ounce of her energy over the years to keep it secret. Fear dropped into her stomach as she thought of all the lives she'd put at risk by failing to do just that. The plane rattled around them, bumping through a patch of light turbulence. She jammed her eyelids shut, trying to staunch the flood of innocent, frightened faces passing across her mind's eye.

"Are you even listening to me?"

"No," Marisol replied, turning back to her racing thoughts.

It wasn't just The Hotel. Jordan had mentioned a handler. That implied knowledge which was just as dangerous. If she thought Sloane was her handler at least one person Marisol cared about was safe. Unfortunately, that meant the other was in far more danger than she could imagine.

"Well, you better start listening," Sloane said, jumping to her feet. She swayed for a heartbeat, the movement of the airplane sending her off balance. "Because you're going to tell me what the hell is going on here. Who is that woman? What does she want from you? Why did she think she could get to you through me? Why does she want to know about a hotel?"

"That's too many questions for me to answer all at once."

Sloane didn't react to Marisol's crooked smile, her jaw set and she said, "Go one by one."

Marisol sighed and let her head fall back. Her neck popped pleasantly but the strain on her shoulders worsened. "Her name's Jordan. She wants information and she wants to hurt me. She thought she could get to me through you because, as you no doubt noticed, she could."

"Why?"

"Because I'm your knight in shining fucking armor." Marisol tried to inject sarcasm into the statement, but she had the sneaking suspicion Sloane knew it was a bluff. "How should I fucking know what she thinks?"

Sloane's eyes bored into her but Marisol didn't look away. She'd spent countless hours dreaming of gazing into those eyes again, but her dreams were much more pleasant than this reality.

"You didn't answer my question about the hotel."

"I didn't answer her question about it either, so unless you're willing to beat me worse than she did, you're out of luck."

They locked eyes again and again Sloane gave in first. She looked away and screamed, balling her bound hands into fists and throwing them into the air. The outburst was unexpected, but Marisol was happy to see the fight coming back into Sloane. She'd need that fight today.

"How can this be happening?" Sloane shouted, her voice echoing in the confined space. She clawed fingers through her hair and paced. "This can't be happening. There are security measures in…"

Blood drained from Sloane's face so quickly Marisol thought she might pass out. She stumbled back to the bank of chairs and dropped into them, shaking hands covering her mouth.

"My guards. Bates and Murphy and… Jesus I never learned his name and he's dead because of me. They're all dead. How could I be so stupid? How could I do this to them?" She turned shining eyes on Marisol and spat words across the cabin. "You! Did you kill Rogers? How many State Police officers did you kill? Were you in their apartment before you came to mine?"

"I didn't kill any of your guards."

The assurance didn't settle her. "How did you get into my building?"

"Back door."

"How?"

"Door knob turned, door swung open, I stepped through."

"Marisol…"

"Don't worry, I shut the door behind me."

"Marisol!"

"What the hell do you want from me?" As Marisol yelled, Sloane's jaw snapped shut but her eyes hardened to chips of blue ice. "You're too predictable. You do the same damn thing all the damn time. You leave Springfield every other Friday night between seven fifteen and eight thirty. You send emails to your friends announcing your arrival. You have your secretary schedule brunches. You wake up at five a.m. and spend thirty minutes on the treadmill. You take every meal in your condo and work until ten p.m. unless you have a friend over for drinks. You're in bed by midnight. You sleep in on Sundays unless your friend stays the night…"

"Enough."

"Brunch is catered by Beatrix or lunch by Bistro Grand. You head back to Springfield in the late afternoon when you have a busy Monday or early evening if you don't. You don't let the State Police into your condo after their initial search. There are two entrances they cover and two they don't know about. I don't think you even know about them."

"I said enough."

"You keep your thermostat at seventy-two during the day and sixty-three overnight. You pay for cable but only use the Internet."

Sloane leaped to her feet again, stalking across the cabin just like Jordan had moments before. "I get it, okay? You're stalking me. You probably know what I wear to bed."

"I'm not stalking you. I'm trying to keep you safe but it's goddamn hard. You're so fucking predictable."

"I know it's my fault!" Tears splashed down her cheeks, but based on the rage twisting her features, they were from anger, not sadness. "I know they're dead because of me. You don't have to rub it in. You think I won't feel their deaths for the rest of my life?"

Sloane's tears made Marisol's anger flare all the more. It was bad enough that she'd nearly gotten herself killed, now she was taking responsibility for those cops' deaths, too. And Jordan thought Sloane was involved in Marisol's secret life. The danger of that was only marginally better than the truth. In the end, it probably wouldn't matter. If Marisol couldn't find a way to break them free, her attempt to save Sloane would have been wasted.

"Can't you just sit in your Governor's Mansion in Springfield and be safe?"

"I didn't realize I was getting myself elected into a cage."

"Of course you were!" Marisol roared, her chest strained against her bonds as she fought to fill her chest with enough air to bellow. "What do you think governors do?"

"Serve the people!" Sloane threw her arms into the air as if it was the most obvious explanation in the world. "Make their state a better place!"

"*Dios*," Marisol breathed, the fight draining from her as her handcuffs bit into her flesh. "You're even more naïve than I thought."

"And just what the fuck is that supposed…"

The hatch burst open and Sloane whipped around to face it. Her knees bent slightly, putting her in a defensive position. Marisol reveled in the flex of her body and the will to survive so apparent in her stance. Maybe the key was to make her angry. Then she seemed more likely to fight back.

"Need to take a leak, Governor?" Jordan asked, looking them both over. It would be impossible for her to miss the adversarial tension in the hold, but Marisol was sure she'd been trying to listen through the door anyway.

"I…" The battle was clear on her features. It had been a long time since either of them had access to facilities, but Sloane was right to mistrust the gesture. Still, she wasn't the type to let her pride rob her of her dignity. She held her head high as she walked to the door.

"What about me?" Marisol asked.

"You can piss on yourself for all I care," Jordan said, slamming the hatch shut.

Marisol didn't need to go, but now was as good a time as any to test her boundaries. Even if she could get free, there was nowhere for her to run while they were still in the air. Better to buy time now with the hopes of cashing out later. She had a lot to think about from her chat with Jordan, but she couldn't help counting every moment Sloane was out of her sight. How long would a trip to the lavatory take? What might happen to her while Marisol wasn't around to protect her?

When Sloane returned, shoved into the hold so roughly she nearly tripped, Jordan did not follow. Sloane crossed to the seats and sat as primly as the circumstances allowed. Something had changed in her face, but Marisol was certain nothing too horrible could have happened in so brief an absence.

She couldn't wait any longer and she blurted, "You okay?"

Sloane nodded, then shook her head and buried her face in her hands. "I can't get their faces out of my mind. I killed them."

"No, you didn't. That assassin killed them."

"And you killed her." There was a steely edge to her words.

"I did."

Sloane looked up and smiled, though it looked like it tasted bitter. "Good."

CHAPTER TWELVE

2005

Marisol sat with her legs folded beneath her on a bare cot in a bare room. Two days' worth of sweat stained her shapeless blue pants and matching shirt. Her hands sat lifeless in her lap. The casual observer might think she was meditating. Just a girl in her mid-twenties, practicing yoga to clear her mind. None of the guards watching her through the tiny square window in her door or the security cameras mounted in the ceiling were that naïve.

What none of them saw was that she was not in this place. Her room was not in a prison surrounded by shouting women. She was in a place of perfect silence. The small rectangular window high on the painted concrete wall held her focus. She stared at the purple-black cloudless night sky and she was there, in that sky, not in her cell.

Because she was not in the room, the door did not open into her world. The man with skin as purple-black as the night sky did not enter. The little red light on the security cameras blinked out in some other room in some other world. When the man spoke, she heard his words in the far, unknowable distance.

Marisol wasn't staring at the sky exactly. She was staring through it. How her mother's eyes stared through her all those years ago from the floor of a dirty apartment in a dirty city in a dirty life. No one knew who she was. Not even Marisol knew who she was. She laughed the first time her lawyer asked for her full name and Social Security number. A five-year-old running for her life doesn't know her Social Security number. She doesn't even know her last name.

She ignored this man when he introduced himself with an obviously false name. She had nothing to think about anymore. Nothing to care about. Her life held too many hours and she didn't feel the need to fill them.

When she didn't respond, he moved across the room and snatched up the flimsy metal chair. The way he moved intrigued Marisol. He moved how she moved. Like a predator. He brought over the chair that Marisol had never sat in despite her endless days alone in the room, but she didn't care. His hands were empty. He had nothing to offer her.

"They tell me you've been in solitary a long time." His voice was higher pitched than she'd expected and quiet. "You don't want to ride out your sentence peacefully?"

She ignored his question the same as she ignored his presence.

"That fits everything I've heard about you," he continued as though they were chatting about the weather. "It must be all you know when you've spent so much of your life fighting. But you're so calm in here alone."

She saw the trap he was laying and chose to watch him build it.

"Maybe you're tired of fighting?" He posed it as a question but didn't wait for her to answer. "No, of course not. You love fighting. You were born to fight."

The paint on the wall above the sink bubbled from decades of carelessly flung water.

"Your resume is very impressive. From nobody to Detroit's most feared criminal all before your twenty-fifth birthday."

Marisol knew that saying even a single word would be her downfall and so she was silent. She learned long ago not to trust anyone, especially if they knew anything about her.

"They caught you for taking out those two idiots," he said, referring to the fools who'd muscled into her territory and had learned the consequences of crossing Marisol Soltero the hard way. "But you were into a lot more than that. You started with minor theft, from what I can tell. The robberies were very sophisticated and you were quiet about moving the goods. That's rare for someone your age. Usually people get flashy and stupid. Not you. Most of the weapons moving through the Midwest either start or end with you. Your competitors have a stunning capacity to go missing, too. I count twenty-seven deaths that can be attributed to you. Something interesting in your rap sheet, though."

Marisol came back to the room slowly. She could tell by the intensity of his pause that the penny was about to drop. She intended to catch it.

"You involve yourself in nearly every avenue of crime, but there is one notable exception. No girls. No link to prostitution or…"

"What do you want from me?"

Marisol's voice sounded odd to her own ears. She hadn't heard it in a long time. It croaked and rasped but it was unmistakably hers. He didn't seem perturbed by the interruption. Too late Marisol realized that he had expected it. It was another trap he was setting while she was distracted by the first. She tucked the trick away in her mind.

"You have a set of skills that I need."

"I don't swing your way, Officer."

So easy to fall back into herself after all these weeks floating alone. Like putting on a favorite shirt. She let herself smile and went back to staring at the wall.

"It's Agent, actually. Agent Anderson."

He was enjoying the game now. She could tell by the spark that lit his hooded eyes. He removed a worn photograph from an inside pocket and set it on the cot beside her. He was silent for a long time. Long enough for Marisol to understand that he was taking control of their game. He wasn't going to speak until she looked at the photo.

When it suited her, Marisol turned her gaze to the picture. It showed a little girl, maybe six or seven, with brightly colored plastic barrettes in her hair and a wide smile. She was utterly unremarkable, just a small Hispanic girl missing two teeth. It might have been a picture of Marisol when she was young, except the girl in the photo was well fed and happy. Marisol had been neither at that age. She had been on the street by then.

"She went missing in Colombia three years ago. Her mother took her to the market, holding her hand the whole time. Someone came by and ripped her away and she never saw her daughter again."

The photograph was in Marisol's hands now and she was studying it intently, though she didn't remember picking it up.

"She was found dead last month in a ditch outside Chicago. There are lots of them. All girls. All young. All…"

"What about it?" Marisol asked, cutting off his words before they could make her feel anything. Before the image of a girl not much older than this one could fully form in her mind. A skinny girl with dusty yellow Converse High Tops and haunted eyes. She held the photo out to him, but his eyes were fixed on her. "Why are you here?"

"I work for an organization that cares very much about this little girl and others like her." He held her gaze and she felt the jaws of the trap snap shut around her foot. "I think you do, too."

"You're wrong."

"Am I?" He crossed his arms and Marisol set the photograph back on the bed. "I know the men who did this well enough to know they would've approached you."

"A lot of people approach me."

He continued like she hadn't spoken, "You aren't a part of this. That means you care."

Laughter escaped before she could stop it. It was without mirth, but it made her chest feel alive for the first time in a long while. "You expect me to go straight."

"I expect exactly the opposite."

She narrowed her eyes at him, her suspicion making her wary again.

"We've been trying to infiltrate these organizations for years. We can't get a cop inside and I'm tired of getting people killed trying."

A glimmer of his plan showed on the horizon and Marisol tracked it as he spoke.

"We can't get a cop into organized crime. We need to get someone in organized crime to be a cop."

"I'm no cop." Images flashed in front of her eyes. Men in blue uniforms beating her friends. Sweet talking the girls. The cops who'd finally arrested her had gentle hands, but their words left wounds she was still licking. "I'll never be a cop."

"Poor choice of words. You'll be far more than a cop." He sat forward, his enthusiasm pressing through his calm façade. "You'll be something entirely new. Unique."

"Enough games. What exactly do you want from me?"

"I want you to go to Chicago. I want you to set up shop there the same way you did in Detroit. I'll offer you limited help with that, and I will…not notice some of the things you do as long as you stay within certain acceptable boundaries."

"Certain acceptable boundaries?"

"My priority is human trafficking." His eyes went to the photograph. "That will be your priority as well. You can fund your work with other enterprises. You get to be yourself, but you also get to help a lot of people. I have a feeling that's something you want to do. Something that would make your mother proud."

A buzzing like a swarm of angry bees filled Marisol's ears. "What do you know about my mother?"

"Likely more than you do."

That wouldn't be hard, since Marisol didn't even know her mother's name. She had the face and the voice of a gentle, kind woman etched into her mind, but she'd just been Mommy to a five-year-old.

"Tell me."

"You can earn it."

Marisol laughed, letting her head drop to her chest. The movement made the muscles in her neck and chest ache. "That's the carrot. Where's the stick?"

He smiled again and the human came back into his eyes. Marisol trusted him even before he spoke. "You're the stick. I won't pretend we don't need you. That I don't need you. You have all the power here and I know enough about your mother to believe you'll use it for good."

She stared at the wall for a long moment. She knew more than anyone else—more than her gang members, more than her lawyer, more than the guards who paced on the edge of her life—that she had nothing left to lose. She'd never had anything to lose. Not from the moment she was born. Marisol looked back at the photograph of the little girl.

"Gabriela." His voice was soft when he spoke the name, like a child making an offering to a priest. "Your mother's name was Gabriela. She was a social worker. The rest you can find out if you cooperate."

No last name. Not enough to do her own research even if she could. Marisol never knew her own last name. She chose a last name by accident as a child on the street.

"Gabriela."

She whispered the name and it felt nice on her lips, but not familiar. It was a pretty name, but not worth dying over.

Before she had a chance to turn him down, he was speaking again. "Ruby, your kind friend from long ago, had a sister. She has a box full of letters from Ruby about a sweet street kid. She's wanted to meet that kid for a long time. Thank her for giving Ruby someone to care about."

Marisol shook her head. She still couldn't hear the Red Hot Chili Peppers without breaking into a blind rage. Ruby's sister might have her same smile and Marisol couldn't handle that.

"Then there's your other friend, Carmen. Don't you want to know who claimed her body?"

She held up her hand but suspected he wouldn't have told her anyway. What could he have said? What could he possibly offer to heal that wound? When Marisol felt a prickling in the corner of her eye, she forced her mind away from Converse High Tops. It wasn't hard to find something else to focus on. Something that made this whole conversation irrelevant. She put one fingertip on the photograph and slid it to the very edge of her cot, as far away from herself as she could manage.

"I'm afraid you're a little late, Agent..." She couldn't remember his made-up name, so she left the sentence blank. "I'd love to accept your help, but I've got a lifetime lease on this cell."

With exceptional care, he tucked the photograph into his inside coat pocket. "The American justice system can be such a tricky thing. How the burden of proof is on the state. How people come forward with new evidence about old cases all the time. When they do, the state is obligated to act. To release anyone who may have been wrongfully convicted. They often have to compensate them for the time they spent in prison."

Marisol smiled at his back as he approached the door. She decided she liked this man quite a lot. Working for him might be fun. Here he was offering her freedom and seed money straight from the government's pocket. She wrapped that knowledge around her like a warm blanket.

"You'll be given an extra set of personal effects when you're released. I trust you'll know what to do with them. Have you ever been to Humboldt Park in Chicago?"

"No."

"You should go. You'll like it there." The lock released with a crack of metal on metal, but he didn't open the door just yet. "You'll like Chicago. You may have been a kingpin in Detroit, but in Chicago? In Chicago, you can be a queen."

CHAPTER THIRTEEN

The cargo hold door squealed slowly open. Jordan stood on the threshold, while finishing a muttered conversation outside. Marisol studied her tension and nervous energy. She seemed keyed up, and that was never a good sign with Jordan. She was too volatile.

It was the final straw that had convinced Marisol to move her years ago. Marisol employed an army of street rats—kids who ran envelopes of cash between couriers. One was a sweet, pre-teen boy who had looked at Marisol like she was a goddess. Jordan had resented his admiration and had promptly made it her mission in life to torment the boy. She and Marisol had spent some time together by then but there had been no question— in Marisol's mind at least—that it was anything more than sex. Jordan, it seemed, had a different idea and she had flexed her muscles by treating Marisol's people like her people.

There was nothing of that unwarranted superiority in her posture now. Based on the timbre of the voice responding to Jordan, Marisol suspected the person on the other side of the door was a man and, more importantly, someone she regarded as an equal. She held her shoulders low and kept her voice even, her biggest tells. Marisol tucked the information away, trying to catch enough of the voice that she might recognize it if she heard it again.

Movement from the corner of her eye revealed Sloane's close attention to the scene as well. There was a fire in her eyes that Marisol was happy to see. Some of the Governor's fear seemed to have dissipated. Now the only question was whether the returning confidence would make her bold or wary. Marisol knew enough of her personality to worry it would make her too bold.

She must have felt Marisol watching her because Sloane met Marisol's eye. Marisol cut her eyes at Jordan, then back to Sloane and gave a sharp shake of her head. Her warning earned her a spike of pain from her sore neck and a sour look from Sloane. Obviously she found Marisol's warning unnecessary and, if her clouded expression and crossed arms were any indicator, probably insulting. Marisol found the venom delightful and smiled widely into Sloane's brewing anger. She'd always known there was more to the unflappably pragmatic politician than she revealed to the public.

With a quick laugh, Jordan ended her conversation and finally entered the hold. Marisol watched her bolt the door as the plane quivered through more turbulence. Jordan tossed a bottle of water at Sloane, who caught it awkwardly. Jordan dragged a chair so close to Marisol that their knees interlocked when she sat down. She leaned in and Marisol smelled coffee on her breath and the sharp, chemical odor of cheap cologne.

"I believe the last time I was here we were chatting about The Hotel."

Marisol leaned back, looking relaxed despite the ropes cutting into her armpits. "You were chatting. I was yawning."

Jordan buried her fist in Marisol's abdomen, pressing all the air up from her diaphragm in a whoosh.

"You were saying about The Hotel?"

Marisol groaned through the pain in her belly. "I'm more of an Airbnb girl myself."

Jordan pulled back her fist again, but didn't strike, scanning Marisol's face. "You aren't ready to talk yet, are you?"

"You figured that out all on your own?"

Jordan sat back in her chair, mimicking Marisol's pose before the punch had doubled her over. She tried and failed to look as confident as Marisol. After a moment's standoff, Jordan glanced over her shoulder toward Sloane. When she looked back, there was a wicked glint in her eye.

Sloane watched her approach but did not show the slightest concern. She met Jordan's gaze with withering disdain before looking away, apparently intent on drinking her water.

"Governor Sloane... May I call you Sabrina?"

"You may call me Governor Sloane."

Jordan's cheeks went slightly pink. Sloane set her water bottle down and crossed her legs, blithely ignoring her captor's attempts to engage. Sloane's bold contempt was enough to make Marisol's mind and eyes wander.

"Well, *Governor Sloane*," Jordan said as she sat, pressing their bodies sickeningly close. "Let's get to know each other, shall we? Want to start with me? No. I didn't think so. How about Marisol? I should warn you she's far more than a common criminal."

"It's true," Marisol spat back. "I'm an exceptional criminal and also a fantastic lay."

Jordan ignored her, stretching her arms wide and letting one fall across Sloane's shoulder like a teenage boy trying to cop a feel.

"Tell me why, Governor, when you were such a powerful SA and took down every crooked cop and drug dealer in Chicago, that you couldn't make anything stick against Marisol."

Sloane shook Jordan's arm off her. "She is extremely well connected."

All three of them felt the weakness of the argument. Marisol knew how hard Sloane had worked to bring charges against her, dogging her every move for years. It wasn't until the distraction of the gubernatorial campaign that she loosened up, and then it was only for a short time. It would have been flattering to be the object of such single-minded attention if Sloane weren't trying to send her back to jail.

"She would need connections to God himself to wriggle out from some of the things she's done." Jordan laughed mirthlessly. "Especially having her life sentence reversed. You know about that, right? Few people make the connection between our Marisol and the Michigan case all those years ago."

"Of course I know. There was new evidence presented that exonerated her."

"Yes. How convenient."

"What exactly are you implying?" There was a hunger in Sloane's eyes now that she finally turned her attention to Jordan. "Do you have information that could…"

"Do I have information?" Jordan's laugh made Marisol's blood run cold. "You may have guessed from our chat earlier that Marisol and I know each other well."

"I gathered that you work for her," Sloane replied, pointedly ignoring the innuendo. "Not exactly something that makes me trust you."

"Oh, we've done more than work together." Jordan leaned in close to Sloane, but kept her eyes on Marisol. "We were lovers."

Marisol laughed, a single note into the close air. "Just 'cause I gave you a piece doesn't mean there was love involved."

The usual look of disgust Sloane reserved just for her shone brighter in the dim light of the cargo bay.

"There wasn't on your side," Jordan admitted. "But I loved you."

"Garbage isn't capable of any emotion. Even love."

"Say what you want," Jordan sneered. "But I was broken for a long time when you sent me away."

"My heart bleeds for you."

"You don't have a heart, Marisol. I figured that out by watching you very closely these last few years. At first I was trying to find a way to get you back. Then I just wanted to know why you left me. After that…well, when I paid attention I noticed some very strange behavior."

"Leaving you isn't strange behavior, Jordan." Marisol's throat went dry even as she tried to laugh through the conversation. "It's perfectly natural to want to be as far from you as possible."

Jordan turned back to Sloane. "Of course my suspicions were shared by others. People with money and power. They required independent verification though."

"Independent verification?" Sloane asked.

"There's a woman Marisol knows. She showed up in Peoria. We had a chat much like the one Marisol and I will have once we're on the ground."

"What woman?" Sloane asked, her voice riding the line between anger and fear.

"Just a piece of garbage we tossed out the window and Marisol picked up. You know the one I'm talking about, don't you? Sweet girl, shame about the birthmark."

The roar erupted from Marisol's lips before she could stop it. She couldn't shake the image of Anna's kind, hesitant smile when Marisol had left her at The Hotel. The smile had been capped by a Port-wine stain birthmark below her right dimple. Marisol flung herself against her bonds, numb to the pain of metal and nylon cutting into her flesh. She bared her teeth and when she spoke blood and spit flew out with her words.

"If you hurt her…"

"You'll do what? Bleed on me?"

Jordan laughed at her joke, but Sloane paled several shades. When Jordan caught sight of her shocked expression, it made her laugh all the harder. She wrapped her arm around Sloane again, pulling her close and speaking conspiratorially into her ear. "You'd be surprised the sort of things a woman will confess when certain *pressures* are applied."

Now it was Marisol's turn to blanch, but her face did not show shock. Rage. Hatred. Frustration, certainly, but not shock. She forced herself to regain her calm, but Jordan must have known she'd scored a point. Marisol took a pair of steadying breaths and reminded herself where she was and what she had to lose.

The door bolt clanked and a man roughly the size of a minivan bent to get through. His muscles strained at the seams of his clothing and his eyes bulged from his ruddy face, the whites jaundiced and his pupils wide. A short fuzz of blond hair covered his scalp and neck, disappearing into the collar of his too-small blazer.

Jordan got to her feet. She shot another meaningful look at Marisol and said, "Speaking of the pressure I applied…"

There was something in the set of his jaw that confirmed Jordan's words. Marisol found herself unable to hold his gaze. She turned and stared hard at the cargo netting and the boxes and bulkhead behind it. The plane shook again and Marisol tried to focus on the reason for the turbulence. Was it a storm or a natural updraft? Possibly from crossing a mountain range? The question of where this plane was headed distracted her from Jordan's implications.

"How could you?" Sloane's words had no effect on Jordan. After a quiet moment she turned her attention to Marisol and her words dripped with regret. "Was she…"

Sloane didn't finish the question and Marisol didn't respond. She just stared at the netting as it swam in and out of focus.

After a few whispered words, the hulk of a man left and Jordan came back over to them. Apparently she'd been listening.

"Was she what, Governor? Marisol's girlfriend? No, she doesn't do relationships."

Marisol had herself under control again. Enough, at least, to shift her attention back to the byplay between the other two. Enough to see the flush on Sloane's cheeks when she countered, "Of course she does. There's that actress."

Jordan shook her head. "She makes more a show with that one than the others, but the truth is she doesn't spend her night with ladies. You have other, more interesting pastimes, don't you Marisol? Shall I tell her the truth?"

"Why don't you go to hell instead?"

Jordan must've known she had the upper hand. Marisol could feel her power slipping away. The only question she had was how much Jordan really knew. Something told her she was about to find out.

"The women, the nightclub, hell, even her businesses— they're all just a cover."

"What kind of cover?"

Jordan had the Governor's complete attention. Sloane was leaning toward her now, rather than the other way around. Marisol could see her chest rising and falling through her clinging dress. She took a moment to appreciate the beauty of that lithe form while she waited for the axe to fall. Jordan didn't give her long to wait.

"The kind that hides her connection to the men who pull her strings back in Washington." She held the silken thread of Marisol's carefully woven life for a split second before she snapped it irrevocably. "Marisol is the NSA's most useful and successful spy."

CHAPTER FOURTEEN

"I don't believe you."

Jordan laughed and Marisol had to admit Sloane's shock was something to see. Governor Sabrina Sloane was not the type of woman to accept such a massive change to her world view readily. She had, after all, spent a good portion of the last ten years hunting down Marisol Soltero, Queen of Humboldt, Chicago's most notorious criminal.

"You really don't, do you? I guess you aren't her handler. Then who..." Jordan's eye flicked back to Marisol, who kept her face as neutral as she could manage. She apparently didn't find what she was looking for there, because she turned back to Sloane. "I didn't believe it at first either, which is why it's such an effective cover. But I have ample evidence. The way I got my information left no doubt she told the truth."

It was Jordan's wicked smile that made Marisol's vision go red and her mind go blank. She fought against her bonds, screaming incoherent obscenities and threats. She didn't feel the pain, even when a thick trickle of blood dripped down her wrists where the handcuffs cut into her flesh. She could tell by the wild panic in Sloane's eyes that she needed to calm down, but all she could think of was frightened women and huddling, shivering girls.

When Marisol finally ran out of energy, she could hear Jordan's mocking laughter. Marisol took a moment to chide herself, then immediately began planning how to take the advantage back. A confident Jordan was dangerous, but a confident Jordan could easily turn into an overconfident Jordan.

"Believe me, Governor, I've done my research."

"Forgive me if I don't believe you."

Jordan paced the small space, her words directed at Sloane and her eyes locked on Marisol's heaving chest. "A Russian businessman living in Chicago who had several women chained in his basement. This was what, four years ago?"

"He was found unconscious in his driveway," Sloane said. "With his basement and computer both unlocked. There were…videos on the hard drive."

"That's right. And then there was a judge in small-town Lisle who extorted defendant's families with the threat of longer prison sentences. Taking bribes to keep their jail time short."

"Judge Alan Owens." Sloane didn't look convinced, even as she recited the details. "He missed several weeks of work after a bad car accident. His clerk found audio recordings in his office while looking for case files."

"Then there's the Black Sun Gang."

"Who?"

"They never made it to your desk, but I remember them. They were a rival Chicago gang. They popped up quickly and got into some of the things we didn't touch. Prostitution. Kidnapping. Extortion. They were wiped out just as quickly as they arrived. Not pushed out, mind you. Wiped out. Every single one of them dead."

"What does any of this…"

"Then, of course, there was Akron Eddie."

Marisol stiffened at the name.

"Who?" Sloane asked impatiently.

"He's out of your jurisdiction, of course," Jordan said, pacing the room. "But he was a particular friend of my employer's. He was quite put out when Eddie showed up in that underground parking deck poked full of holes. Know anything about that, Marisol?"

"Never much cared for Ohio."

Jordan shook her head as she walked. "Eddie was a piece of shit, but..."

"So you were friends."

Jordan continued as though Marisol hadn't spoken, "But he was good at moving our merchandise. Nobody could sell a girl like Eddie."

"Fuck you."

"I saw his body after you popped him," Jordan said. "It looked personal."

Marisol kept her features carefully neutral, but she knew where she'd made her mistake. Fucking Akron Eddie. She had enjoyed killing him and it must've shown. Only someone like Jordan, who enjoyed causing pain, could have spotted the one time Marisol let her guard down.

"You're implying that Marisol had something to do with all of these?" Sloane sat like a statue, her back rigid and her distaste clear. "I'll remind you that several of those matters were my work."

"Yes, but they are just the appetizer." Jordan came and sat in front of Marisol again. "I'm curious, though, about other events."

She stared into Marisol's eyes and Marisol stared back.

"I'm very interested in certain events involving Governor Sloane. Those puzzle me."

Marisol held her body as though she were frozen.

"I assure you, there are no events that involve Marisol Soltero and me."

Marisol had no intention of telling Jordan about their weekend and clearly Sloane was going to act like it never happened. As much as denying it burned Marisol, at least Sloane was smart enough to keep it secret from Jordan.

"No? Are you sure about that?"

Sloane finally looked over at Marisol, searching for some answer, but Marisol was not about to give it.

Jordan was all too willing to continue playing storyteller. "You've made a good many enemies through the years, Governor. Did you know that?"

"All State's Attorneys and politicians have enemies."

"Yours seem rather inclined to assassinate you."

"You're the only person who's ever tried to."

"Not true. Quite a few of them have tried. Marisol here has saved your life six times."

Sloane's voice was barely audible as she croaked, "Nonsense."

"In fact," Jordan said, ignoring Sloane's skepticism. "If there is one thing Marisol does particularly well, it's stop people from killing you."

Sloane just stared at Marisol, her mouth agape. She seemed to search for something in Marisol's face, but she'd spent years making sure there was never anything there for anyone to read.

As the silence stretched, Marisol decided it was time to have a little more fun. "Who knew I had such a big fan? Maybe I shouldn't have given you such a hard time about fucking like a dead fish."

The veneer of confidence cracked and Jordan's eyes went wild. She shot to her feet, her flimsy chair skittering across the metal floor. She slammed her fist into Marisol's midriff, maniacal laughter bursting covering Marisol's grunt of pain.

Over and over again her fists pummeled Marisol's abdomen, each blow landing like a freight train. Marisol kept her eyes locked on Sloane's—horrified and disbelieving—to keep herself distracted from the hurt.

After what felt like a lifetime, a loud knock at the door stopped Jordan short. She straightened, gasping for breath. She turned on her heel and marched out of the hold.

Marisol relaxed her stomach muscles one at a time, inch by agonizing inch, trying not to vomit and ruin her bravado. She stared at the blank wall, forcing herself to breathe evenly. It was harder than she'd anticipated and she felt sweat collecting on her brow. She took an experimental breath and her muscles immediately seized again. She dropped her head, closing her eyes as she breathed. With each deep breath the pain lessened, or she became used to it—she wasn't sure which.

"Marisol…"

She shook her head and winced, stopping Sloane's question before it began. While she fought a second round of nausea, Marisol distracted herself by focusing on the feel of the plane descending. The pitch of the engine changed dramatically and she felt the pull of gravity as they pitched forward. Their destination was fast approaching. They were running out of time.

"Was all of that true?"

Marisol refused to look up, even though Sloane's voice held a quality Marisol had never heard before. It was curious and inquisitive, but also quiet. Unsure.

Marisol weighed her options. It seemed easier to fall back on old habits, so she responded through clenched teeth, "Yes, it's all true. Jordan's worthless in bed. I should've just faked it to get out of there."

"You know that's not what I meant."

"Are you sure about that, Governor? Don't worry, it was before you and me."

Sloane let out a frustrated huff and turned her head away, staring at the closed door. Marisol allowed herself a moment to admire the graceful lines of her long neck and the waving beauty of her hair.

When Sloane didn't look back, Marisol gave in. She sighed, defeated, and said, "Look, I…I'm not a fucking saint. Don't expect so much of me. I will admit that I am…more than just the Queen of Humboldt."

Sloane sprang to her feet, making Marisol tense, pressing her body back into the chair at the unexpected movement. She marched across to the chair Jordan had used, throwing herself into it and getting right into Marisol's personal space.

"Answer my question."

"I don't…"

"Did you set up that Russian businessman?"

Sloane's tone was so commanding, Marisol nodded before she knew what she was doing.

Sloane's shoulders relaxed a fraction, but she didn't let up. "Did you expose Judge Owens's blackmail?"

Marisol locked her gaze and nodded. She'd spent so long hiding who she was, she couldn't quite bring herself to say the words out loud. Still, it seemed pointless to deny those facts from Sloane when they were already out in the open.

"That Eddie person? And the gang?"

Marisol hesitated. It was one thing to admit exposing criminals, it was quite another to confess to killing dozens of people. Sloane looked at her with a defiance she knew would not be satisfied until she had the truth. Marisol nodded deliberately.

Sloane asked in a small voice, "Have you really saved my life six times?"

"Governor..."

"Please...just answer me."

"No." Sloane's confusion was evident, so Marisol continued. "Counting tonight and your Inauguration Day, I've saved your life eight times."

Sloane's brows knitted in confusion and she opened her mouth to inquire further, but the door slammed open, banging against the wall. Just as Jordan and the Hulk marched in, she sprang back out of the chair as though she'd been electrocuted.

"Time to move Marisol and I think we need the rabid dog leashed for this journey."

Hulk marched toward Sloane, whose eyes filled with terror as she backed away. He reached out and she yelped.

"Get your hands off her you..."

Marisol couldn't concoct an eloquent insult for him. The plane tilted sharply as they descended, but Jordan's hand was coming up much faster than the ground beneath them. The cloth in her palm covered Marisol's mouth and nose, filling her senses with a suffocating sweetness. She didn't have a chance to cough. She didn't have a chance to shout or jerk away. She breathed reflexively and her vision blurred and shivered at the edges. Another breath and blackness enveloped her.

CHAPTER FIFTEEN

2015

Sloane waited behind the wheel of her car until she could take a full breath. She'd known how hard this would be and she thought she'd prepared herself, but clearly she hadn't done as thorough a job as she'd intended. She'd stayed in her office late last night, reviewing her notes for today's deposition. She had wasted nearly an hour staring into the distance, chewing on her pen and remembering in exquisite detail a particular weekend five years ago. She gave herself a pep talk. When her thoughts had wandered back to a hotel room bathed in moonlight she'd changed the pep talk into a reprimand.

It hadn't worked. She'd dreamed of Marisol last night. That hadn't happened in over a year. The very thought made her ill. It was bad enough that she'd been tricked into bed. The knowledge that she'd shared those intimacies with a murderous criminal enraged her again. Once she was able to channel that disgust away from herself to where it belonged, she wrenched her car door open and marched toward her office.

Just as she had expected, Marisol Soltero had arrived in the conference room before her. Once again she cursed the circumstances that brought the two of them together like this. Facing Marisol again in a crowded courtroom would have been infinitely simpler, but nothing with Marisol was simple. She'd refused to give her evidence in court, inventing an excuse to be out of the country during trial. Had she been the defendant, Sloane could have issued a subpoena, but Marisol was only a witness. A key witness and likely just as guilty as the man on trial, but until she could prove some crime, Sloane would have to settle for this deposition rather than a chance to spar with her in open court.

Sloane took one last, shuddering breath and steeled herself to see that face again. Marisol sat across the table with her lawyer, a snake in a suit if there ever was one. Marisol was lounging in her chair, blithely ignoring the court reporter and the defendant's attorney.

"State's Attorney Sloane," Marisol's lawyer said, hopping to his feet and buttoning his triple-breasted suit jacket. "How kind of you to join us."

Sloane shook his damp palm and promptly turned her attention to defending counsel. If the other lawyer was a snake, this man was a rat. His hair was oiled down, pulled back from his high forehead and his sliver of a nose. His small, puckered mouth didn't move as he shook her hand. At least his client wasn't present for the proceedings. Though it was a defendant's right to face his accuser, Brent Willow had declined. Sloane would like to have believed he was intimidated by her, but it was equally possible he didn't want to face off against Marisol. By all accounts he, like so many other rivals, was terrified of her.

Marisol neither stood nor offered her hand. Sloane kept her eyes carefully averted from her broad shoulders and full lips.

"Thank you both for your promptness," Sloane replied, pleased to see that ignoring the rebuke made Marisol's lawyer squint his beady eyes.

She further provoked them by turning her attention to the court reporter, checking to see all his needs were met before they began. She set an antagonistic air by spending just enough time with him to ensure the two lawyers were forced to return to their seats.

The only hitch in her plan was Marisol, who remained unruffled. In fact, as Sloane took the seat directly across from her, Marisol smiled, her right cheek dimpling ever so slightly. She'd noticed the dimple the day they'd met. While they'd shared an overpriced bottle of wine, she'd pressed her cheek against that dimple and whispered an invitation to the hotel a block over.

But then that day in court, Detective Krone had filled her in on the woman sitting with the reporters, the woman with whom she'd just spent a weekend. She'd been sick over how much more than wine they'd shared.

Sloane cleared her throat, forcing her attention away from Marisol. "Thank you for taking the time to offer this deposition, Ms. Soltero. I'm sure the sworn testimony you provide will be of value to the prosecution."

"Please," she sat forward, the dimple deepening with her widening smile. "Call me Marisol."

Sloane had no intention of doing so. As far as she was concerned, this deposition was merely a warmup for putting Marisol back in prison. The more evidence she gathered on this case, the more Marisol's name and business interests popped up. It wasn't a coincidence and Sloane would prove it. She of all people knew how nasty Marisol was. Far worse than the defendant. She would put Marisol in jail, and she would use every weapon she could find to do it. Brent Willow, nothing more than a low-rent pimp, was going to jail first, however.

"Before we begin, I'd just like to express again that the court would prefer in-person testimony at the trial."

"As much as I strive to assist the State's Attorney's office, I'm afraid Dominique's trip cannot be rescheduled. She's a Goodwill Ambassador for the UN."

The name sent a cube of ice into Sloane's gut. Marisol could brag about her famous girlfriend's status all she wanted. Sloane was certain the trip had nothing to do with goodwill and everything to do with removing Marisol from Illinois during the trial. Her palms itched to throw this smug liar in jail, but she'd covered her tracks far too well for that. At the very least Sloane could get rid of a pimp who "employed" women kidnapped from their home countries, transported to the United States illegally and sold into sexual slavery.

"Shall we get started?" Willow's Defense Counsel asked.

With a nod to her assistant manning the camera, Sloane began the deposition. She was barely through the standard swearing in and discussion of the usual stipulations when she knew this would be a long day. Beyond the fact that Marisol sat her chair like the queen she pretended to be, her lawyer was sharper than Sloane had anticipated. While Defense Counsel was antagonistic from the outset, Marisol's lawyer was perfectly calm. The longer the discussion continued, the surer Sloane was of two things—first that she would annihilate Defense Counsel at trial and, second, that she was happy not to be facing Marisol's lawyer.

Formalities out of the way, Sloane started in on Marisol. She was careful not to show her strategy too early, but Marisol was almost as slippery as her lawyer.

"How are you acquainted with the defendant, Ms. Soltero?"

Sloane focused on the tapping of keys from the court reporter rather than the wide smile across from her. "I expect I know him the same way you do. He has a reputation."

"A reputation as what?"

"Objection. Hearsay," Defense Counsel shouted.

"I'll rephrase. Are you involved in any business dealing with the accused?"

Marisol leaned back in her chair, crossing an ankle over her knee. "I don't know of any businesses he runs. Do you?"

"I'll ask the questions. Mr. Willow has not been cooperative with the authorities but…"

"Criminals can be so stubborn sometimes," Marisol drawled.

"You would certainly know about that, Ms. Soltero."

"That's out of bounds," Marisol's attorney piped up.

"I've reformed, Mrs. Sloane."

"That's Ms. Sloane."

"Is it?" Marisol leaned over the table, her voice coming like a purr. "Even better."

Marisol just wanted to get a reaction and Sloane's cheeks had provided one. She thought of faking anger to cover the blush but that wasn't playing to her plan. Marisol was only trying to provoke her. Surely she knew Sloane wasn't married just as well as Sloane knew about Dominique and all the other women Marisol flaunted around town.

"We've subpoenaed Mr. Willow's phone records." She slid a thick folder across the table. "He's used your courier service quite often in the last eighteen months, then he abruptly stopped. Can you explain that?"

"We were a new business," Marisol replied, flipping open the folder and scanning the pages. Bright yellow highlighter stood out against the white. "We took all the work we could get. Now we're more established, we can be more selective with our clientele."

"And why was Mr. Willow deselected?"

"He seemed unsavory." She slid the folder back across the table, but Defense Counsel shot out of his chair to intercept it. "It made me uncomfortable. I have excellent instincts, wouldn't you say, Ms. Sloane?"

"Let's discuss the nature of your business."

An hour of grilling passed and Marisol wove a pretty picture of her business dealings. No matter how Sloane quizzed her, she was no closer to revealing the illicit nature of her work. That there was an illicit nature, Sloane was certain. Everyone in Chicago knew Marisol had a hand in every criminal activity there was. Not just her dealings with Willow. He was scum, but low-level scum. Sloane's last case as ASA involved the importation of stolen goods. Marisol's name had come up, but Sloane couldn't pin anything on her then either. For it to happen again now was too much of a coincidence.

"How do these questions pertain to the case?" Marisol's attorney asked. "My client is not on trial."

"Ms. Soltero seems to have an inordinate number of business dealings in countries that have problems with human trafficking. Do you have a response?" Sloane asked, forcing herself not to scowl.

"I didn't hear a question."

"Did I accurately describe the nature of your business holdings?"

"You did," Marisol sat forward, tapping her finger against the rim of her untouched water glass. "I also have an inordinate number of business dealings in countries with mountain ranges. Surely you don't think I plan to smuggle the Andes into Chicago?"

"What do you smuggle into Chicago?"

"Objection," Marisol's attorney roared, looking flustered for the first time. "My client is not on trial."

"Of course," Sloane replied, her chest warming with every bead of sweat popping up on the attorney's brow. "I'll strike the question."

"I think that concludes our participation in this farce," he said, rising from his chair, fists planted on the tabletop. "I should've known your only intention was to harass my client."

He was out the door before the camera was off, but Marisol took her time straightening her jacket and rounding the table. Sloane watched Defense Counsel scuttle out, and so Marisol was almost on top of her before she realized it.

"This was fun, Sabrina." Her smile and silky voice were more suited to a dimly lit bar than a conference room. "We should do it again sometime."

"Given your criminal behavior, I have no doubt that we will. And don't you dare use my first name."

After the court reporter slipped past them out the door, Marisol leaned in closer. "There was a time when you liked hearing me whisper your name. You liked it even better when I shouted it. Have you forgotten? Want a reminder?"

As though she could've forgotten. For a heartbeat the rustle of stiff cotton sheets and muffled laughter filled her senses but vanished just as quickly.

"Have you forgotten what it's like in prison? Want a reminder?"

Marisol's face turned to stone in an instant and Sloane felt a flash of involuntary regret. Marisol's voice didn't purr when she said, "He's off the street and the women are safe. Isn't that enough for you?"

Sloane's pulse pounded so loudly she could barely hear herself ask, "What do you know about the women?"

"I know they don't have to work for that scum anymore."

"They're missing," Sloane said, grabbing Marisol's arm and feeling soft leather bruise in her grip. "Every one of them. If you know where they are..."

"I don't," Marisol said, a shadow passing over her deep brown eyes so quickly Sloane wondered if it was a trick of the light.

"Marisol..."

She smirked, leaning in so close now Sloane could smell the leather of her jacket and the musk of her cologne. It was the same one she'd worn to the courthouse that day. "You called me Marisol."

Sloane slammed the door behind her exit, but it wasn't quite loud enough to drown out Marisol's low chuckle.

CHAPTER SIXTEEN

The heat was intense. It was a thick, heavy heat that clung to Marisol's skin and made her mind sluggish as she forced herself to consciousness. She could tell from the temperature that they weren't in Chicago. She tried to calculate how long they'd been in the air. Seven hours? Eight? She'd been unconscious for part of the journey so it was hard to tell. With that much air time they could be almost anywhere, but the humidity and the vehicle's rattle from poorly maintained roads suggested South America.

Brakes squealed. A burst of well-articulated Spanish and an aroma that made Marisol's mouth water filtered in through the open window. Chicken and potato and the headiness of warm cream, but there was something else, too. A grassy, herbaceous scent that evaporated as soon as the vehicle ground back into motion and the smell of dusty, dried mud took its place.

The smells and sounds poked at her brain, pressing her to pinpoint them and what they all meant. It only took a quiet moment to remember. An assignment from Washington four, maybe five years ago. She had been tracking down the source of a steady stream of kidnapped girls being smuggled into the country through Canada. Dominique had been a goodwill ambassador for UNICEF, and Washington had arranged a tour.

They had spent a week in Bogota and the surrounding, impoverished communities. That was where they'd tried *ajiaco*, the most popular dish in the city. A soup of chicken, corn and three types of potatoes. It was similar to soups served in Peru and Cuba, but the Colombian version used an herb the others didn't. Guascas, a weed everywhere except the Colombian Andes. Dominique had loved the soup so much that they'd eaten it nearly every night. It had provided the protein and carbs Marisol had needed for her late-night reconnaissance.

So, she now understood they had been flown to Colombia. Probably around Bogota. Maybe even guests of the very people Marisol had failed to track down on that trip years ago. She'd dreamed of getting another shot at them, but this wasn't exactly what she'd had in mind.

The vehicle hit a particularly deep rut and Marisol's cheek and shoulder, already twisted uncomfortably, smacked into the bare metal floor. She opened her eyes to find Sloane staring into them, fear dripping from her face like her sweat in the oppressive heat. They were lying in the back of a cargo van.

Marisol's body ached, particularly her torso. She tried to move her chin and relieve some of the pressure on her face, but the moment she lifted her head, the van floor bounced up to meet it with bruising force. She couldn't suppress a groan as her temple throbbed. She stretched her face muscles, opening her mouth and wiggling her jaw and eyebrows. The beating had been some time ago, but everywhere hurt.

"Getting knocked out like this is probably bad for my health. I hope that anesthesia they're using is FDA approved." Sloane's look of fear turned to annoyance in the blink of an eye. Marisol winked at her. "Still, better than getting punched out. The bruises definitely aren't good for my gorgeous looks."

It was obvious Sloane's hands had been tied for the journey too. Marisol followed a bead of sweat as it trickled down her long neck to dampen the high neck of her dress. Her eyes did not stop there. Sloane wasn't oblivious to the inspection, especially considering how thorough it was, but it was possible she shifted her body to lessen her muscle strain rather than to hide her body.

"How can you joke at a time like this?" Sloane hissed, keeping her voice low.

Marisol rolled onto her back to relieve the cramp in her shoulders. The moment she moved, she regretted it. They'd replaced the handcuffs with rope while she was out and bound her tied hands to her ankles with one end looped around her neck. Rolling onto her back had pulled the noose tight, choking her. They'd hogtied her and done a thorough job of it. She managed to roll over and relieve the pressure on her throat, but it was a painful lesson. She took several long breaths before looking back into Sloane's startled face.

Marisol forced a dry laugh from her aching throat. "If I don't make jokes now, I might not get the chance."

"I don't know where the plane landed. We were in a hangar when they tied us up and tossed us in this van." Her eyelids drooped as she looked around the confines of the vehicle. When she blinked, her eyelids didn't seem to want to open again, but she kept prattling on in a hiss. "We've only been on the road a few minutes. I don't know where we are, but I don't think we're in the US anymore. Not unless they flew in circles before they landed."

"We're in Colombia."

"How do you know?"

"I know everything."

Sloane scowled at her and didn't respond. She looked like she barely had the energy to breathe. Marisol tried to guess how long the Governor had been awake and decided it had to be a day and a half at least. Sloane was an early riser and it had been late when they'd been captured. Apart from the forced nap the tranquilizer provided, she'd been awake and on edge for far too long.

Marisol scanned the van compartment, looking for something to help them. It only took a moment to see there was nothing. There wasn't as much as a loose carpet nail for her to use on the ropes. The cab was closed off by a makeshift barrier of poorly cut plywood. There was a break at floor level on the driver's side, Sloane's side, but Marisol lay at the wrong angle to see through.

"What are we going to do?"

Sloane's voice was so drained, Marisol stopped her inspection to look over. To her surprise, she saw tears floating on the red rims of Sloane's eyes. Marisol bit the side of her cheek hard to control her response.

"You're going to take a nap."

"What? You can't possibly expect me to fall asleep right now."

"You're exhausted and completely spent." The gentle concern surprised even Marisol, so she lightened her tone. "I need you at full strength when an opportunity presents itself. Understand, *amante*?"

Sloane was quiet for a long moment, but there was a set to her jaw again. She nodded and closed her eyes. Silence filled the van for a few minutes as Marisol wished Sloane to sleep. Soon enough, her shoulders began to rise and fall in a regular rhythm and Marisol's whole body relaxed.

Marisol was used to being a lone wolf. She had underlings and bodyguards and even a few friends, but the work that meant the most to her she did alone. Only herself to worry about. She needed that feeling now. The luxury of not having to school her features. Not having to play a part. It was exhausting to be so many things to so many people.

She needed time to think. To plan and strategize. Unfortunately, though she had time now, Sloane being in her space was more than a little distracting. Instead of forming a plan, she watched Sloane's face melt slowly into serenity. Watched her chest rise and fall beneath the clinging dress providing incontrovertible proof that Sloane was alive and here, close enough for Marisol to touch.

Sloane's long eyelashes fluttered open and Marisol quickly slipped her mask back on. In a voice draped in sleep, she asked, "You saved my life on Inauguration Day?"

She was adorable, childlike in her drowsy innocence. Marisol couldn't help the light, bubbly feeling in her chest. She let herself chuckle low and there may even have been the hint of a blush on her brown cheeks.

"Yeah. I did."

Sloane's eyes slid shut and she drifted back off to sleep. Something that sounded very much like "Thank you" escaped her barely parted lips, but Marisol forced herself to believe it was just a sigh bordering on a snore.

Marisol sighed herself, making her decision. She had to see what she was dealing with. It was easier said than done, but she steeled herself and pushed hard off her shoulder. The choking began the moment she moved and didn't lessen as she finally struggled to her knees. Bright white lights popped in front of her eyes, so she pushed herself over into a better position.

She landed almost exactly as she wanted to, mere inches from Sloane, and gasped for air. Underneath their mingled sweat, Marisol could still catch the faint scent of Sloane's expensive perfume—lilies and peaches. Marisol's body quaked at the closeness, her oxygen-starved mind begging to close the gap between their bodies. Before she lost all control, Marisol stretched her neck back, peering through the gap in the barrier.

The view of the cab wasn't great. Just the underside of the steering column and a few boots, but that was all she needed. The keyring dangling from the ignition had a rabbit's foot keychain dyed a bright, garish purple. She counted four pairs of boots, one set significantly smaller than the others. Jordan had always been ridiculously proud of her tiny feet. So they hadn't been passed off to someone else. Jordan was still in here. Whether or not she was still in charge, she was a known enemy and that meant Marisol had an advantage, however small, over one of her kidnappers.

Marisol relaxed her tortured neck and closed her eyes. She allowed herself one long moment of watching the quiet rhythm of Sloane's breathing. To feel the heat rising from her skin. She had to get back to the other side of the van. If she was out of place when they opened the doors, Jordan would know she'd been up to something. Worse, she might suspect the reason Marisol spent so much time rescuing Sloane. Her words and actions wouldn't betray her, but her body might. It responded to Sloane in a way it never had to anyone else. Still, she couldn't make herself give up this wonderful spot. Not yet.

Just when she was about to force herself back to her knees, the van slowed and then shuddered to a halt. Over the ticking of the engine, Marisol heard a voice that made her blood go cold. The van ground back into motion and the voice disappeared.

It was all she needed to know who was pulling Jordan's strings. The man who had brought Marisol and Dominique to Bogota before. How Jordan had gotten involved in all of this, Marisol couldn't imagine. He was out of Jordan's league by several million degrees, but he was here and it all started to make sense. She didn't have a lot of time.

Marisol allowed herself one more deep breath of Sloane's scent before forcing herself to her knees. She tried to be quick, but her fatigue was nearly fatal. She slipped into a half-crouch, her weight falling forward, and she couldn't correct it. The noose dug into her neck, cutting off her air.

She couldn't breathe. She couldn't move. She couldn't think. Darkness started closing in from all sides, taking her vision down to a narrow tunnel. At the end of that tunnel was the still peaceful, still sleeping face of Sabrina Sloane. Her consciousness slipped and her mind thought, for the briefest moment, that at least she would die looking into that face.

The van hit a deep pothole and Marisol tumbled onto her side. She opened her mouth as wide as it would go and sucked in all the air around her. Life flowed back into her. Her vision cleared by degrees, letting the world back in.

Exhaustion took her then. Her eyes rolled back and she fell into a deep sleep. As the world faded away, Sloane's last, sleepy question echoed in her delirious mind.

CHAPTER SEVENTEEN

2019

Letting her steps roll quietly from heel to toe, Marisol crept across the dark warehouse. The floor was concrete, and her boots would slap loudly if she wasn't careful. Clouds covered the half moon, the skylights and high windows barely glowing. She'd kept one eye closed while picking the lock, preserving her night vision.

Despite her careful pace, she was able to cross the warehouse in little time. She'd watched an endless stream of tractor trailers leave earlier in the day, so she wasn't surprised to find the place empty. It wasn't in the greatest area of town and she worried about squatters. Once she reached the stairs at the far end of the building she was confident that she was alone in the freezing warehouse.

Moving with more speed and only slightly more sound, she climbed the stairs. The lock on the office door was pathetic, just a rattling knob with a three-pin lock. Marisol had it open in fifteen seconds. Sweeping the room with her dim flashlight, she took a moment to slide aside a tile from the drop ceiling.

The computer on the desk was a red herring. It was a dusty old box that would probably take an hour to boot up. She doubted it held more than shipping manifests and preinstalled solitaire. If her intel on these guys was anywhere close to accurate, the solitaire got a lot more play than the paperwork. They were so sloppy she sneered at even calling them businessmen.

The file cabinet against the back wall was a little more helpful. Nothing was incriminating by itself, but she got a few useful names and addresses. She didn't have anything personal against them, so maybe she'd just send them to prison rather than kill them. Killing was so messy and, after all, she hadn't gotten the ex-State's Attorney a parting gift yet.

The flashlight played across a cheap folding table. A familiar map caught her eye. Incredulous, she studied the papers. The maps, diagrams and reports were all familiar. Marisol had a copy of them herself, and she had come by them at great expense and trouble. Unlike her copies, these were Chicago Police Department originals.

Marisol's phone vibrated insistently in her pocket. She flipped off her flashlight and pulled herself into the ceiling. The warehouse door banged open just as she slid the tile back into place, leaving a barely perceptible gap. Balanced on a ceiling beam above the office, she could hear the men climbing the stairs to the office. Among the rafters was an open skylight a hundred yards away, but she waited to see if these jokers had anything interesting to say. They chatted like TV-show bad guys, complete with dick jokes and long, obviously untrue stories about women they'd picked up in bars. Marisol was about to leave when the office door opened again and the laughter died.

Marisol couldn't see the newcomer's face, but there was no mistaking those orthotic black sneakers and black polyester uniform pants. Whoever this guy was, Marisol hadn't seen any cops with these guys before.

The energy in the room changed the minute the cop walked in. It had been jovial but now it was a full-on sausage party. Marisol could feel the testosterone in the air as each party tried to act like the one in charge. The goons won out in the end. The uniform proved the cop wasn't a detective and the gangsters were the old-fashioned type—greasy hair, cheap suits and enough pinky rings and gold crosses to fill a pawn shop.

Passing over the money was perfunctory. The zipper on the duffel screeched as the cop yanked the bag open. His hosts bristled as he counted his fee, but he didn't linger over it. One of the suits dropped a cell phone into the center of the flimsy table, turning on the speaker. It rang twice before the other end picked up.

Marisol could barely believe their stupidity as they laid out their plan for the morning. The cop marked all the security points on a map with a red felt pen and the questions from the phone could only be from the main shooter. They were either incredibly bold or incredibly stupid to try such a straightforward, simplistic plan.

Marisol didn't have to see the map to deduce which building would house the assassin. It was the most obvious, of course. The cops had assigned a single spotter supporting a single sniper. Unfortunately, he'd be a sitting duck, since his spotter was currently plotting his death in an abandoned warehouse. This cop didn't seem to worry about killing one of his brothers in blue.

"Just as long as the bitch Governor gets what's coming to her."

He spat the words with enough poison for Marisol to guess he hadn't always worn polyester uniform pants. He was probably one of the crooked detectives Sloane had taken down over the years as SA. Marisol smiled, thinking of her marching into this cop's office while he had sat smugly behind his desk. She wished she could have seen Sloane wipe the smile off his face.

The meeting ended just as abruptly as it had begun. The moment the cell phone went dark the mood shifted. The tension broke. They had their plan and, after hearing the whole thing, Marisol had to admit it was a good one. One that she couldn't stop on her own.

"*Hijo de puta*," she whispered, her breath puffing out in little frozen clouds.

"You wanna drink, friend?"

The cop had been heading for the door, the duffel bag in his fist. He accepted a Peroni from a chubby, swarthy hand and tipped it back to the ceiling. His eyes followed the bottle, staring directly through the crack in the ceiling tile. He would have seen Marisol's face looking back at him, but she'd jumped before his fingers touched the cold glass.

The ceiling tile snapped across the cop's face, shattering the bottle as he fell. Marisol landed with the heel of one boot on the worn carpet floor and the other driving through his collar bone. It crunched under her weight and he screamed. Her chrome-plated Colt was spitting fire as she turned, grinding her boot into his broken bone. None of the men had a chance to pull their weapons before they died.

Marisol slipped the phone from the table and memorized the last number in the call log before dropping it in her pocket. She'd toss it into the river as soon as she had a chance.

Job done, she headed for the door. She almost laughed to see the cop, trying to drag himself toward the closest body. He should've brought his own gun, but maybe they took it from him when he arrived. It didn't matter now. Marisol ejected the clip from her Colt and inserted a fresh one as she walked. The cop stopped moving and looked into her face.

"I know who you are."

"*Felicidades.*"

"You're Marisol Soltero."

Marisol stopped in front of him, watching his wild eyes dart around the room.

"You should be on our side. You should want Sloane dead as much as we do."

"I should want that, shouldn't I?"

She raised the pistol and squeezed the trigger twice in quick succession. The pool of blood from his head spread slowly across the carpet, filling in the impression where her boot landed as she walked past his body. His duffel bag vanished along with his killer.

"Gray," she spoke low and slow into the phone after he picked up on the first ring. "I need you to track a number for me."

After he took down the phone number and repeated it back to her, she let it fall out of her head. She didn't have room in her memory for the phone number of a man who'd be dead in less than 24 hours.

"Everything okay, boss? Something you need me to do?"

She heard the question in his voice. It'd been there a while now and she'd ignored it. He was careful to show that he wouldn't push, but she again considered bringing him in. She'd trusted him with her own life since she was sixteen. He'd come right back like a loyal hound after she'd been released from prison. Made the move to Chicago without hesitation. He was loyal, but she couldn't trust him with more than her own life. Not yet.

"Just get me the info. Everything else I can take care of on my own."

She hung up and jumped onto her bike. She didn't have a lot of time. The sun was already rising. As she drove downtown, she passed crews putting out crowd control barriers.

Gray's call didn't come until late morning, but it was enough time. She was already in her storage unit, gathering the supplies she needed. In the end, all she really wanted for this was a silencer, a lot of bullets and a calm manner. The hardware she had in abundance. Acquiring the calm demeanor was how she'd spent her night. Therese was always a good candidate to clear her head. She'd pulled Marisol into her place by the lapels of her leather jacket and sleepily pointed her toward the shower two hours later.

Now Marisol's hand was steady.

She left it until the last minute to enter the building. Too early and she would arouse suspicion. Thanks to the map last night, she knew where everyone was. She slipped from room to room in the dark office building, taking them out one at a time. Some of the marked rooms were empty thanks to her efforts last night and most of the men she did find were wary. Probably wondering where their bosses were, but not worried enough to call the whole thing off.

As the sounds of cheering grew closer and closer Marisol moved like a panther. Her silencer spat so many times that it glowed.

The only challenge came on the roof. She found the police sniper near the door, his eyes glazed and frost forming on his skin. Thanks to Gray, she now knew who her target was. A former Army sniper who liked to brag about his kills from Iraq and Afghanistan. He didn't hide the fact that he'd despised them for their religion and hadn't cared if his "enemies" were women and children. He wasn't a fan of women in the military, women in the workforce or, especially, women in office. Marisol deeply enjoyed sliding up behind him and depositing three bullets into the base of his skull. She set her Glock beside his knee, careful to avoid touching the hot metal.

When she got back to the lobby the noise of the crowd was earsplitting. A group of suspiciously muscled cleaners marched through the glass doors as she approached the entrance. Their uniforms were a little too generic and they flared out in a triangle the moment space allowed. The man in front looked Marisol dead in the eye, winked and walked past without a word. Washington had come through after all. By sweeping up after her, awkward questions were kept to a minimum.

Marisol slipped unnoticed into the crowd, which was practically pulsating with joy. Most of those around her were women, their cheeks gleaming in the cold. Marisol eased through them, dropping her gloves on the ground as she went. She wore a black windbreaker over her normal leather jacket, and that too went onto the sticky pavement. It would all be haphazardly cleaned as soon as the Inauguration was over.

Once she'd forced her way to the front of the crowd, she handed a ticket over and dropped into her assigned folding chair near the stage. Sloane emerged a moment later, climbing the stage as some faceless bureaucrat spoke of her historic election win.

Marisol had eyes only for Sloane, who wore a rare smile. Marisol knew she had already been in Springfield for weeks, working 14-hour days to clean up the mess left by the trust-fund moron she was replacing. She could see the weariness around Sloane's fiery eyes and the exhaustion in the way she forced her chin high. She could see it, but she suspected no one else could. She watched Sloane's every move, guessing with each gesture what she was thinking.

The speech ended a moment later and Sloane made a circuit around the stage, waving high and pumping her fist to the crowd. They ate it up. Even Marisol felt her heartrate pick up.

When the crowds began to disperse, Marisol pushed through them to the back of the empty stage. A crew of cold, grumpy workers was already taking down the bunting and coiling up audio cables. She put her back to a tree trunk to catch her breath, waiting until the park was unoccupied before disappearing back into the shadows.

CHAPTER EIGHTEEN

The van jerked to a halt, jarring Sloane into panicked wakefulness. Exhaustion had allowed her to doze, but it was a restless, uneasy sleep slashed with nightmares. At one point she had half woken to the feel of Marisol's body close to hers. A heady mixture of musky skin and the sharp tang of sweat had filled her nostrils and made her head spin, but she hadn't been able to force her eyes open. She had drifted into sleep again, chased by the vague sense of being watched, and her dreams were troubled by phantoms.

The monsters who wrenched open the van doors, however, were all too real. Rough hands grabbed at her arms and her hair, dragging her painfully across the metal van floor and dumping her onto dusty, hard-packed earth. Hulk pulled her up by her bound hands, and she couldn't bite back a scream of pain as her shoulder twisted under her weight. The giant turned from her, finding more entertainment in the back of the van.

Sloane was pleased to see the fight Marisol was putting up. Two men, who together barely matched the Hulk's muscle, struggled to shift Marisol as she kicked and bit them. They spoke to each other in rapid Spanish, and she spat back at them in the same language. Marisol's eyes rolled like a wild beast, spit flying from her lips as she fought to twist her body around. The noose around her neck cut deeply into her skin, leaving red slashes in it's wake.

Eventually Sloane realized Marisol was looking for her. As her eyes searched the van's interior, there was a glaze over them that Sloane had seen before—when Marisol had come crashing through the ceiling of her apartment building like a devil falling from heaven at the exact right moment. This time Sloane responded as she hadn't been able to then.

She took two steps toward the van when the Hulk's massive fist twisted into her hair, yanking painfully at her scalp. She yelped in pain again, though not as loudly this time, it was enough to catch Marisol's attention. She stopped thrashing and their eyes locked. For a heartbeat, Sloane felt like she was safe. Then a coarse bag that smelled like rotten cabbages dropped over her head and she was in darkness.

Unseeing now, Sloane kept still and silent, trying to understand what was happening. With the zing of a knife her hands dropped free. She hissed as her shoulders and neck, sore from so long in the awkward tied position, relaxed. Blood flowed back into her cold fingertips, bringing pins and needles with them. Strong hands gripped both of her upper arms and she felt the very solid form of her captor uncomfortably close behind her. She knew better than to attempt escape. She wouldn't make it five feet before they caught her. She didn't want to think what Jordan would do to punish her. Instead she breathed through the pain as quietly as she could and listened.

The heavy thump nearby was followed by a gurgle and a good deal of angry spluttering. Sloane remembered how Marisol had been tied, with her feet lashed to the noose around her neck, and knew that they dumped her out of the van in a way that was choking her. Panic flooded back into Sloane. Marisol may not be an ally, but she was the only person nearby who was not an enemy. If for no other reason than that, Sloane needed her to survive.

A knife zinged again and the choking ceased. It was replaced by an almost imperceptible groaning. Sloane still felt the pins and needles in her shoulders and hands. How much worse must that be for Marisol, who had been tied much tighter and more awkwardly and had been bashed repeatedly over the course of the long flight. Her body must be in agony.

"You gotta see this."

Hulk ripped off Sloane's hood, taking a fair amount of hair with it. As her eyes adjusted to the light, Sloane saw what they were all laughing at. Marisol also had a sack over her head, and there was a long rope hanging behind it. Her feet were free now, but her hands were still tied behind her back. She'd fallen onto her stomach and the men were dragging her across the dusty ground by the noose.

Marisol scrambled with her heavy boots to get purchase on the loose dirt, but the men dragged her like a dog on a leash toward a ramshackle structure with rusted aluminum siding. Marisol stumbled blindly to her knees, only for the men to yank her back down. Sloane sucked in her breath as she watched Marisol's chin make contact with the ground and her head snap back.

The hood dropped back over Sloane's face, muffling her captors' inane laughter and Marisol's animal grunts. Sloane walked with her back ramrod straight and her steps measured. These people wouldn't see her cower or crawl. Hulk made it difficult. He pushed her forward then held her back, trying to make her steps falter. Her bare feet stubbed the rough ground.

Once, when she nearly tumbled forward out of his grip, she let out a squeak of fear. Hulk pulled her body sickeningly close to his own and growled into her ear, "You scared, little one? You should be. Once the boss gets what she wants, you're all mine."

Sloane felt the sweat trail down her neck, grateful for the hood covering her shocked face. She hadn't thought of what would happen after Marisol broke, but now she realized they would never let her go. If Marisol's guess about their location was correct, they had managed to get her out of the country. Any likelihood of release was slim. She chose not to think about it, pushing fear from her mind with the practiced ease of a seasoned leader.

They didn't take her far. When the heat dropped away, she knew they'd marched her into the ramshackle building.

Sloane heard them toss Marisol to the ground. The dirt floor shook with the impact and a moment later the hood was yanked off again. Before her eyes could adjust, an open palm slammed between her shoulder blades and she fell hard. She landed on top of the squirming, sweat-soaked body of Marisol, who froze the moment their bodies met.

"Stay here and keep your damn mouths shut."

Hulk spat onto the ground beside Sloane's head. Her face was inches from Marisol, her labored breathing making both their bodies rise and fall. Fresh blood oozed from Marisol's right nostril. Sloane could smell the copper-penny reek of it. She couldn't help her lip curling in disgust, but instantly regretted the sneer. For the briefest flash, when their eyes met, she saw pain wash across Marisol's gaze. Her gut twisted at the vulnerability of it, but it was gone in a flash, replaced with a lewd waggle of eyebrows and the faintest grinding of Marisol's hips up into hers.

"Like it up there, Governor? We could make it a permanent position if you want."

This time she did not regret her distaste. She scrambled to her feet, putting as much distance between them as she could manage.

"You're right, we'll save the fun for later. I am a little tied up at the moment."

Sloane turned away, examining her surroundings rather than the involuntary swoop of her stomach when Marisol's pelvis had brushed against hers. They were in a shed, closed into a small room. The corrugated walls had holes letting in pinpricks of bright afternoon light. A single bare bulb hung from one of the rafters, leaving the room in semidarkness.

The whole place smelled foul, like rotten meat and old sweat. Her gut told her nothing good would happen to them here. The filth of too many days clung to her and she wished she was home safe in her condo where she could bathe in cool, clean water.

A metal door in the far wall banged open, slamming against the wall. Hulk marched in and threw a pair of battered metal bowls onto the ground.

"Eat, bitches. Get some sleep if you want, we won't need you for a while yet. Just keep quiet or I'll make sure you're *real* quiet."

His massive hands twitched, the fingers flexing as though he yearned to wrap them around someone's neck, but he marched back through the door, hauling it shut behind him. It took Sloane a long time to make her hands stop shaking.

Marisol struggled to her knees, swaying noticeably. Rather than try to stand, she crawled toward the bowls, her hands still tied behind her back and the noose trailing through the dirt. Sloane followed at a distance, her stomach roaring with hunger. It fell silent the moment she saw the contents of the bowls.

Dirty, soggy rice the color of old mud drooped flaccidly in the bowl. Flies swarmed around the food but seemed just as hesitant as Sloane to get too close.

Sloane put a hand to her mouth. "I think I'm going to be sick."

Marisol squatted in front of one of the bowls, her back heaving as she sucked in air. She looked over her shoulder at Sloane, who could see exhaustion and pain etched into her face.

"How long's it been since you ate?"

Sloane tried to think. She'd had a long week and had left Springfield for the solace of her Chicago apartment without stopping for dinner. She thought she'd had lunch at her desk, but couldn't remember what it had been. They'd been in the plane a long time, though she couldn't be sure how long since the heady mixture of fear and adrenaline made her internal clock as twisted as a Dali painting.

"I don't know. A day maybe?"

"Eat."

"You have to be kidding."

"You need your strength."

"For what?"

Marisol's only answer was a hard stare that made Sloane immediately reach for the bowl. She raised it to her nose reluctantly and sniffed. It smelled far worse than it looked and Sloane now realized it was served to them in a cheap dog bowl. Eventually she dipped her fingers into the soggy mess and brought a pile close to her lips. She shook it to get a fly off and closed her eyes.

It tasted even worse than it smelled. It took everything in her to swallow. Once she was sure it was staying down, she took her bowl and slumped against the wall. She tested another bite, keeping her eyes averted from the bowl as best she could. It was just as bad as the first, but at least now she was slightly more comfortable.

Marisol grinned from the center of the room, then turned back to the bowl. Hands still tied, she bent over, dropping her face into it and biting mouthfuls. She looked like a junkyard dog, scavenging trash. Not for the first time, Sloane marveled at the distance between them.

Marisol swallowed noisily and shrugged, a few grains of rice falling off her chin back into the bowl. "Pretty nasty, but I've had worse."

"Yes, I imagine you have."

The words were out before Sloane could catch them, and she felt the heat on her cheeks as the smile slid off Marisol's face.

"Not you though, huh?" Her next words were mumbled like an accusation. "Always had a silver spoon."

Sloane had to admit the accusation was completely true. She shoved another handful of rice into her mouth and chewed purposefully. "I suppose you expect me to apologize for not being an orphan?"

Marisol stiffened midbite. She didn't look up and she didn't blush, but Sloane could tell she was shocked and maybe even a little embarrassed. It occurred to her that Marisol wasn't aware how much Sloane knew about her past. After the trial that sent Willow to jail, Sloane had requested regular updates to Marisol's file. She had a responsibility to the people of Chicago to clean up the streets and that included removing Marisol Soltero from them.

She never forgot how Marisol had used her and lied to her, but her stomach had fluttered with anticipation each time the file returned to her desk. She certainly hadn't expected to be moved, but the bleak tale would be enough to move anyone. There wasn't much about her early life apart from a few minor shoplifting and pick-pocketing offenses. References to her association with a prostitute ended when the woman had been found dead in her cheap hotel room. Detroit PD had dragged Marisol in for questioning, and, reading between the lines, had suspected she knew something about the crime.

Sloane reminded herself, while she watched Marisol drop to take another mouthful from the bowl, that she'd lived a hard life. Working the case back in her office, Sloane had thought she was little better than a ticking time bomb. Seeing her adapt to the incredible situation they found themselves in here, she realized how heartless that assessment had been. Then there was the story about Marisol saving her life. Apparently repeatedly. She still hadn't worked out whether she believed it. Or whether she believed any of the rest of it.

The moment the last of the rice was in her mouth, Sloane dropped the bowl, letting it clatter against the beaten earth floor.

"Are you really a spy?"

"I wouldn't be a very good spy if I blabbed about my work to the first pretty face, now would I?"

Sloane chose to ignore the flirting since it was so obviously a trick. "That's not an answer."

"No," Marisol said as she straightened and tried to flex her shoulders. The ropes prevented most of her movements and she winced. "It isn't."

"You've lied to me before."

"And I'll probably lie to you again."

This was going nowhere and Sloane growled her next question, "Why have you saved my life so often? If you really have."

Someone pounded on the door, making Sloane jump. Shouting outside seemed to indicate that they were being too loud. She got up and moved across the room on tiptoe. She may not like Marisol's company, but it was preferable to Hulk.

"Answer my question," she said in a whisper, kneeling next to Marisol.

"If I answer you this once, will you stop asking?"

"No."

Marisol laughed, deep and throaty and they were so close that Sloane swore she felt the vibrations of it. "You're an exasperating woman, Brin."

Sloane held her body very still. Leave it to Marisol to take a liberty she had neither asked for nor been granted. As the holder of one of the most esteemed offices in the nation, few people dreamt of calling her by anything but her last name or title. She had come to think of herself as Sloane when she thought of herself at all, and those occasions were increasingly rare. None of her friends even called her Sabrina. No one but Marisol had ever called her Brin, and that only once but she had to admit she found the name beautiful. It was the sort of nickname she might like to have if she ever allowed herself space to be someone other than her job. To hear Marisol speak to her so familiarly, especially after all they'd shared so long ago, made her stomach flip.

"The night before your Inauguration I was…working on something else."

"Spying?"

"I told you I'm only answering one question."

She didn't like the evasion, but she'd interviewed enough witnesses to know she often got more if she let them speak freely.

"I found some documents. Maps, schedules, diagrams. They all had the official police seals."

"Impossible."

"You sure about that?"

The more she thought about it, the less sure she became. She hadn't made many friends during her time in the Prosecutor's office. Powerful men didn't like being challenged and, in many cases, prosecuted by, a woman. Particularly a gay woman who wasn't impressed by them, whether they wore a suit or a badge.

"I can't imagine someone in the State Police hated me enough to kill me."

"Not state. Chicago PD."

Sloane's stomach dropped. It couldn't be true, could it? The day had been such a blur, but, if she focused, she could remember a few things were out of the ordinary. Whispered conferences at the periphery of her vision. State Police and Chicago Police officers shouting at each other, squaring off in that aggressively masculine way that usually indicated powerlessness. And during her speech, right in the center of the crowd at her feet, Marisol with her arm around her on-again, off-again girlfriend. Had she really been fresh from the murder of potential assassins?

For a long, heart-stopping moment, Marisol stared into her eyes. There was an honesty in her gaze, a look that Sloane knew should make her wary. She kept quiet, pleading for answers with her silence, but the moment shattered and clouds of deceit rolled back across Marisol's eyes.

"We should take his advice," Marisol said in a low, even tone. "Get some sleep."

Sloane nearly said she wasn't tired. She nearly shouted in frustration. She nearly reached out and shook Marisol by the shoulders, demanding answers. Instead, she squeezed her hands tightly together until her fury receded. It was the feeling of helplessness that annoyed her as much as Marisol's dodge. Neither of them would be helped by a temper tantrum. So she nodded and backed up several feet, lying down at a respectable distance from her fellow prisoner.

Rather than lie down herself, Marisol rolled onto her back and worked her booted feet around the rope binding her hands. Her hands now in front of her, she hopped to her feet with surprising agility and prowled the perimeter of the room, stopping for a long moment to listen at the door and even longer to squint through one of the holes in the exterior wall. When she arrived at an alcove in the far corner, she sneered and swatted at the air, thick with flies. With a sigh she delved into the closet-sized room, her face even more disgusted when she emerged a short while later, buttoning her pants.

"I wouldn't trust the water in the sink, but at least the toilet flushes."

Suddenly Sloane was very happy she'd been escorted to the airplane's bathroom because she had no intention of using the facilities here. Marisol gave the room one last, searching look before stepping back through her bonds. Sloane almost asked why she'd do such a thing, but even she could recognize the benefits of hiding how easy it had been for her to gain some freedom.

She watched Marisol lie down, face first in the dirt and try to adjust her body to as natural a position as her bonds allowed. Within moments she was fast asleep, the rhythmic rise and fall of her back and the darting movements of her eyes under closed lids proof that this, at least, was no act.

Sloane watched her for a long time. The lines of weariness and pain slowly smoothed out until she almost looked like a child. A little girl at peace. Remembering Marisol's file and the cold, matter-of-fact information *Mother: unknown. Father: unknown. Siblings: unknown. Next of kin: unknown*, Sloane realized for the first time that this woman had never been an ordinary little girl. The thought made her want to cry, but she forced herself not to.

More than pity, more than fear, the sight of Marisol at peace made her heart thud. Now that she had time to study the lines of that extraordinary body, the feelings she'd fought since waking up in bed next to this gorgeous woman wearing a cocky half-smile bubbled to the surface again.

She finally admitted to herself that it was not just Marisol's beauty. It was one thing when Marisol was a criminal. A killer. Now there was a chance Marisol was more than that, something better, and Sloane found herself both terrified and excited by the prospect. Whole new possibilities opened up.

Possibilities, yes, but not exactly new ones. Sloane had been told once before that Marisol was more than just an outlaw.

CHAPTER NINETEEN

2019

Leaning on the railing of the second-floor balcony, Sloane did her best not to sneer at the sight below her. The Grand Ballroom of The Drake Hotel was bursting with tuxedos and diamonds. Just Sloane and nine hundred of her closest friends drinking ridiculously expensive champagne paid for by the reelection fund her campaign manager had started the day after her landslide victory.

A particularly loud burst of laughter carried through the room. Sloane groaned as she recognized her campaign manager's fake laugh. She'd thought she'd be able to take a break after the campaign was over. She had been naïve. If anything, the campaigning had only just begun. The thought left a bitter taste that couldn't be washed away with the glass of delicious Chardonnay she was nursing.

In truth she didn't really know these people and she certainly didn't like them, but they'd believed in her message enough to put her in office and she owed them a night of fake smiles and glad-handing. She didn't have to like it though. If it were up to Sloane, there would be no party. The parade this afternoon and the speeches after her swearing in had been bad enough.

She had already begun the work of being Governor, despite the protests of her friends who'd insisted she'd have enough long nights in the coming four years. She had work to do cleaning up the state government. As far as she was concerned, that job had started the moment she'd been elected, and it didn't require a black tie gala. It required long hours and hard work.

A waft of something that may have been cologne or may have been perfume caught her attention as she felt the heat of another person close behind her. Too close.

"You look like you need a friend."

The voice was familiar, but it took her a moment to place. The magnetic presence was far easier for Sloane to identify. She turned and had to bite the inside of her cheek to keep from gasping. It had been four years since she'd deposed Marisol in the Willow matter, ten since their weekend together, but Sloane's mind had been on her many times since. Now Marisol stood before her in a perfectly tailored tuxedo and thin black bow tie that somehow managed to be entirely feminine and entirely, deliciously androgynous at the same time. The sight of her was a thrill, but the echo of her voice was nothing short of mesmerizing. Like honey-laced whiskey.

Sloane allowed herself ten or twelve seconds to drink it in before turning away. "Not from the likes of you, Marisol Soltero."

Sloane felt the woman's deep chuckle more than heard it. "I'm honored you remember me, Governor."

"I keep tabs on all the lawbreakers in my town." The answer was smooth enough, but Sloane cursed herself for letting that slip. It wouldn't do her former office any good for Marisol to know she was being watched. "Which makes me wonder how you got into my party. I don't recall inviting any criminals."

With a sneer that matched Sloane's, Marisol came and stood next to her, surveying the crowd.

"You're fooling yourself if you think that. But you're too smart to really believe they're all upstanding citizens."

Sloane's gaze was drawn to a man moving through the crowd below her. A defense attorney of the worst sort. He knew his clients were guilty and used every nasty trick he could to have them acquitted. They paid him in blood money and he cashed every check without remorse. She'd investigated him but couldn't find anything unlawful. It was men like him who had inspired her to run for office and close the loopholes they walked through every day. Sloane had to admit his presence proved Marisol right.

Marisol raised her glass and Sloane's nostrils filled with the mingled scents of rich, musky cologne and smoky, well-aged tequila. She was reminded that Marisol had expensive tastes. Tastes that were funded by activities far more obviously criminal than the attorney's. She stood up and turned to face Marisol.

"How did you get in here?"

"I have an influential friend."

Dominique Levy. Of course. The actress had been very supportive of Sloane's campaign. She was also involved with Marisol again if the tabloid pictures of the two of them were any judge.

"Then you should rejoin that friend."

Marisol moved closer, bringing the musky cologne and her heat with her. Sloane's senses swam as Marisol brought her lips to within inches of her face. She could smell the tequila on Marisol's breath, but it wasn't the alcohol that made Sloane's mouth water. There was something of the liquor in Marisol's eyes, too. Her pupils were wide in the balcony's low light.

"I am capable of keeping more than one friend happy, Governor Sloane."

Sloane hated herself for the heat that spread across her cheeks and even more for the images that raced through her mind. She forced herself to replace those images with others. Photographs of crime scenes attributed to this woman. Hate burned away the lust. It gave her voice a sharp edge.

"You are a criminal. A killer. Probably a pimp. The idea that I would lower myself to…"

"Thinking of lowering yourself, eh?" Marisol pressed her body forward, so close barely a particle of air could squeeze between her tailored tux and Sloane's shimmering, floor-length gown. "I had a little something else in mind. You see…"

Sloane didn't trust herself to hear the end of that suggestion. She spun on her heel and marched away with as much dignity as her watery knees would allow. Marisol's low, throaty chuckle followed her down the stairs. Sloane didn't dare turn around, even to level a warning glare, since she knew her cheeks were burning redder than ever.

She made straight for the women's bathroom, slamming the heel of her palm into the carved mahogany door. It swung easily on well-greased hinges, revealing the plush red chairs and settees of the sitting area. The moment the door swung shut behind her, she vented her anger with such force she nearly spilled her wine.

"Of all the insufferable, arrogant…"

Sloane stopped dead when she saw a pale calf peeking out from the slit in a pearl grey evening gown. Dominique Levy sat on a low stool in front of a vanity, a tube of bright-red lipstick hovering halfway to her lips. She had the elegant poise of a classic movie star paired with the confidence of an older woman who knew herself. There was a twinkle in her eye as she finally applied the lipstick and Sloane knew her embarrassment showed plainly on her face.

"I'm sorry. I thought I was alone."

Dominique dropped the lipstick into her clutch and snapped it shut before swiveling to face her. "Not at all. I think perhaps I'm the one who owes you an apology."

"I don't know what you…"

"I take it you've met my 'plus one.'"

"We… Yes. I ran into her."

She laughed and the sound was like church bells ringing in the distance. "You must forgive Marisol. She is…very confident."

Sloane let a million responses die on her tongue. All she could think of was the smoke and pepper from tequila on Marisol's breath. Anger flared unexpectedly and her words burst out before she could stop them.

"How could you associate with that woman? She's...She's..."

"She is quite special, I agree."

"I was going to say unbearable. Crass. Despicable."

In a fluid movement that defied her sky-high heels Dominque rose to her feet. She showed no hint of annoyance at Sloane's characterization. She smiled languidly, not unlike Marisol. Sloane found herself wondering if they'd developed the similar expression over lazy mornings in bed and a spark of jealousy flared before she could douse it.

"Marisol is a woman of great honor. She simply...expresses it differently than we might," Dominque said as Sloane emptied her glass. The wine had warmed considerably and the bouquet of butter and honeysuckle bloomed in her mouth. "You may come to hold her in as high esteem as I do one day."

Sloane lowered the glass, snorting into it at the thought.

"I doubt that very much."

CHAPTER TWENTY

Gentle fingers ran through Marisol's hair. She didn't remember her dream, but there was a lingering sweetness in her mind that was stoked by the caress. She tried to remember the last time she'd received such an intimate touch and came up blank. She kept her eyes closed and let herself believe it was Sloane touching her like this.

The happy bubble of hope burst when Jordan whispered in her ear. "Marisol? Wake up."

"I wasn't asleep."

"Shh!" Jordan's fingers pressed against her lips. "I don't want her to wake up. I want a minute alone with you."

Marisol opened her eyes to find Jordan's face alarmingly close. She'd lain next to Marisol, the lengths of their bodies almost touching. The daylight glowing through the holes in the walls was gone and the room was much colder. She tried unsuccessfully to hold back her shiver.

"Just hear me out," Jordan whispered.

She looked quieter. Calmer now they had landed. For a moment in the muted light from the bare bulb overhead, she looked like the young, relatively innocent woman Marisol had taken to bed all those years ago. The stench of dirt and old blood reminded her pointedly that Jordan was not, in fact, that woman.

"Start talking," Marisol growled.

"My boss'll be here soon. You know who he is?"

"Why don't you tell me?"

"He's not a nice guy."

"You don't say."

"Around here they call him *El Obispo*."

Her earlier guess confirmed, she decided to play dumb and get as much from Jordan as she could. "The Bishop? He's a priest?"

"God, no," she hissed, her eyes darting around the room. "He likes to wear those starched collars so he looks like a priest, but no one would ever confuse him for someone holy. Around here, when anyone sees him coming, they start praying."

Marisol swallowed hard. She'd heard the stories. Not from Jordan or those in Washington, but from women in The Hotel. Most of them spoke about him in terrified whispers, the way Jordan was now, but she wasn't crying. And had no scars.

"Why would you work for a man like that?" Marisol asked. "I never asked you to…"

"I know you didn't," Jordan said in a rush, her hand moving to Marisol's shoulder. "I know how you feel about people who treat women like that."

"People like you."

"I don't want to do it." When Marisol rolled her eyes Jordan gripped her shoulder and rushed on. "I don't want to. I never wanted to. I was just so hurt when you rejected me. I wanted to be the one thing you hated above everything else. I…took my anger too far. I know that now, but it's too late, baby."

Marisol remembered with a stab of guilt how young Jordan had been when they'd been involved. The damage a person suffers at twenty-one can last a lifetime. "It isn't too late, Jordan. It's never too late."

"You don't know the things I've done."

Jordan wouldn't meet her eye. She looked to the ground between them and stroked Marisol's leather jacket.

"I've done worse, you know that. I've done terrible things."

"Not like this."

"No. Not like this." Marisol waited for Jordan to look at her again, to show her eyes, but they remained fixed on the floor. "But you can stop."

Jordan shook her head, jerking it awkwardly before dropping her forehead. "It's too late for me, but it's not too late for you."

There was the hook. Marisol had known it would come, but it was still disappointing how obvious Jordan was.

"It's not too late for her either," Jordan continued, jerking her chin at Sloane sleeping in the shadows.

"You'll let her go?"

Jordan looked up finally and Marisol saw the lie in her eyes. She'd been smart to avoid eye contact before. There was nothing subtle about her, but Marisol would play this game to the end regardless.

"What would it take?"

"Who's your handler?" Jordan licked her lips and they glistened in the dark. "Who's your contact in Chicago?"

"You thought it was Sloane. Why would you let her go if you think she's my handler?"

"It's obvious she isn't and honestly I don't care why you keep saving her. I just need information, Marisol, and I need it fast."

"What's the hurry?"

"He's coming," Jordan hissed, her eyes sparkling, the reflection of the bare bulb shining in her pupils. "He's coming and he'll hurt you worse than me if you haven't talked."

More likely he'd hurt Jordan, Marisol thought. She was always the loyal hound. Always looking for her owner to pat her head. When Marisol held her leash she craved praise, but there had never been the danger of a beating. The Bishop wouldn't hesitate to punish her if she couldn't get what he wanted.

Marisol pushed her face close to Jordan's, close enough to hear her breath hitch. "You've already hurt me, Jordan. What's the difference?"

"The difference is I won't skin you alive," she barked before moderating her volume. "I can't keep you safe once he gets here. You have to tell me before that."

"No," Marisol said. She was done with this game.

"Please, Marisol. You don't have to suffer." She shot a quick glance over her shoulder, scanning the room. "You tell me what I want to know and I'll let Sloane go. I'll even save your precious women."

"Bullshit."

"You have my word. I won't tell him where The Hotel is. I'll go there myself and burn it to the ground."

"Letting them go first?"

Her hesitation spoke louder than her words. "Of course."

"Jordan?" Marisol said, furrowing her brows as she whispered the name.

"Yes?"

"Go fuck yourself. You're scum. You're worse than scum. You're a lying, betraying, worthless bitch. I wouldn't make a deal with you for a pack of gum."

Silence roared through the room as Jordan stared hard at her. Her jaw repetitively clenched and unclenched, her teeth grinding together audibly in the close quarters. Marisol waited for her to explode, for her fury to erupt as it had on the plane, but it never did. After a moment of fuming she rolled away from Marisol and pushed to her feet. Marisol watched her walk slowly away. She didn't even slam the door.

"That was pretty stupid." Sloane's voice floated through the darkness a moment later.

"Yeah, well, I'm good at stupid," Marisol said before rolling back over on her stomach and closing her eyes. She needed to rest, but she couldn't help think about what would happen when the door opened again.

"It was also very brave," Sloane said.

Marisol tried to think of a pithy reply, but the shock of praise from Sabrina Sloane kept her silent long enough to drift off to sleep.

CHAPTER TWENTY-ONE

Marisol was awake and struggling to sit before the metal door smashed into the wall. She didn't have time to get upright before Jordan and her goons were on her. Jordan got to her first, grabbing a fistful of Marisol's choppy hair and yanking hard, ruining her precarious balance. The roots of her hair held and the strain went to her neck. Marisol bit down hard to keep from screaming in pain.

"Get to your feet!"

The look of abject terror in Sloane's wide eyes made Marisol swallow the insult she longed to hurl at Jordan. Instead, she focused on getting oxygen into her lungs. Jordan's goons appeared on either side of Marisol, hauling her up by her shoulders. Jordan kept firm hold of her hair, pulling her torso down at an awkward angle to keep her from fighting back while the men cut the rope around her wrists. She needn't have bothered. The moment her arms swung to a more natural position, pain tore through Marisol's muscles. Blood pounded back into areas long neglected and she couldn't hold back her scream. If the restricted blood flow was painful, its rapid return was agony.

A sturdy nylon rope around her wrists replaced the zip ties, this time in front of her body. Whichever man did the job was either a sailor or a seasoned kidnapper, his movements swift and practiced. Marisol watched with detached resignation as one of them tossed a length of rope over an exposed rafter. With a coiled thwack of a snake falling from a tree it fell back to the floor. The other man stabbed the point of a meat hook through the twists of rope separating her wrists. She knew what was coming and had an instant to prepare before they reeled in the free end of the rope. With savage speed they hauled her off her feet. Her toes were barely scraping the floor, just holding up a portion of her body weight, when they tied off around a cleat on the nearest pillar. As they released the rope it slipped a little, providing a few more inches of slack. She allowed her body weight to pull the rope taut. They used another length of rope to bind her ankles together.

Their job done, the two men disappeared. The room rang with sudden silence, the three women now its only inhabitants.

Jordan prowled forward, a holster slung low on her slim hips containing a very familiar Colt. Marisol growled at the sight. No one threatened her. Certainly not with her own gun. Jordan stopped a few feet from Marisol, dropping an unzipped duffel bag at her feet. It clattered ominously, spilling its contents onto the floor.

Marisol spotted a Bowie knife the size of her forearm, its double-edged tip gleaming. It was the least intimidating item in the bag. She also saw meat hooks in a variety of sizes, from a large hook like the one holding her off the ground to one no larger than a crocodile's claw. A worn baseball bat was stained a sickening red-black. And then there was the dental equipment. She took a deep, calming breath and prepared her body for what was to come.

Jordan's eyes moved with glee across the implements. She finally settled on a long black cylinder with a pair of protruding metal points. She tested the weight in her hand before taking a single, loping stride forward and jamming the points into Marisol's unprotected side.

She wasn't able to give voice to her agony. The electricity of the cattle prod locked her jaw. Sloane screamed for her. Marisol did not let it register. Instead, she forced her face to remain blank and tried not to let her eyes roll. Her vision was blank white but she could still feel Jordan's delight at her pain. It ran through the room a frequency below the crackle of electricity.

Jordan yanked the prod away, leaving a pair of scorched holes in Marisol's shirt. With all the strength she could muster, Marisol held her knees firm, refusing them permission to buckle. A thin cord of saliva slipped from her slack bottom lip, but her legs held.

"Tell me about The Hotel."

Marisol's lungs burned with the effort to inflate and deflate. She tested a deep breath and found it held. She blew it out slowly.

"You may as well kill me, Jordan."

"No!"

"Shut up, Governor!" Eyes wide, Jordan's head whipped around at Sloane's outburst. "If it were up to me, you would be dead twice over. Don't make me warn you again."

Marisol spoke her next words to Sloane. "I won't say a word, so you might as well let me die."

Jordan grabbed her jaw, pinching painfully at her lips. "Don't worry, Marisol. You'll die. You'll die and I'll be the one to do it. But that won't be for a long time yet. We have hours, maybe days to play. You'll talk. Trust me, you will."

She spent some time showing Marisol exactly what those hours would be like. The cattle prod was only the start, though she used it long enough to leave Marisol drooping on the hook, her shoulders straining terribly. She moved on to the bat after that, softening up the fleshy places on Marisol's body without breaking bone. Marisol had no doubt that would come later.

It wasn't until Jordan discarded the bat in favor of one of the smaller meat hooks that Sloane spoke up again. Jordan nestled the handle against her palm. The hook, a good eight or ten inches long, rested between her fingers like a sadistic middle finger. She slid the wicked point along Marisol's neck, leaving a shallow scratch that oozed a single droplet of blood. The moment the point came to rest against Marisol's windpipe, Sloane shot to her feet.

"Stop it! Stop it, you'll kill her!"

Marisol shouted before Jordan could, "Sit down!"

Whether it was shock that the admonition came from Marisol or numbness from all that she had seen, Sloane stood frozen as Jordan leapt across the room. Sloane cowered as Jordan brandished the hook at her, but she did not cry and she did not sit down.

"Didn't I warn you to shut up? Do you doubt that I'll kill you to get what I want? I thought by now you would be..."

"Tell me what you're talking about." Sloane's voice wasn't quite steady, but it carried an undeniable note of confidence. "If I'm going to die over this hotel, I want to know what it is."

Marisol tried to tell her to be quiet, but her strength gave out and all she could manage was a gurgling groan as she slumped forward, supported only by the hook through her bindings. It didn't hurt nearly as much as she thought it would. Her foot swayed drunkenly, propped on the toe of her boot like a wobbly ballet dancer *en pointe*.

"You want to know, do you?" Jordan smirked and pressed the curve of the hook into Sloane's cheek. "Shall I tell her, Marisol?"

"Go fuck yourself."

Jordan chuckled and slid the cold steel across Sloane's cheek. "I think that's a yes, don't you, Governor?"

"Just tell me."

Sloane kept her eyes fixed on Marisol's slumped form, ostentatiously ignoring the woman standing so close to her. Marisol didn't waste energy trying to meet her eye. She couldn't muster the strength to protest as Jordan revealed the secrets she had sworn her life to protect.

"After I'm done with Marisol, I'll teach you some respect," Jordan said, caressing Sloane's cheek again with the hook. "But for now, I think it'll do Marisol good to know just how many of her secrets I know. It might inspire her to share the rest. The Hotel is a safe house. A place to hide people."

"What people? Who are they hiding from?"

"People who think they have free will, even though they belong to someone else." Jordan paced around behind Sloane, slapping the flat end of the meat hook into her open palm. "You see my employer is a businessman."

Marisol couldn't keep silent anymore, but there was only air enough in her lungs to croak. "He's a monster."

"Yes, he is. I gave you the chance to get out of this without ever meeting him, but you had to be stubborn."

Sloane's forehead furrowed, "This hotel belongs to your employer?"

"No, only those inside it belong to him. As I said, he's a businessman. Certain wealthy individuals require a product. He provides it to them for a price."

"You're talking about women." Marisol finally managed to raise her head, her eyes slicing through Jordan without touching her. "Girls. They aren't things to be bought and sold."

Jordan ignored her, dropping her lips close to Sloane's ear. "Like any good businessman, he keeps close eye on his inventory. That inventory started to disappear when no one was looking."

Marisol's eyes finally landed on Sloane. She saw something in the woman's face. She looked impressed or, at the very least, not disgusted. Marisol was unaccountably pleased at the prospect that Sloane might respect her. At the moment she could not allow herself to get lost in the warm feeling of it, so she held it away from her. Tucked it aside until later. She let her head fall again.

"We heard rumors. Someone who came and stole the merchandise. Took them away to a safe place until they could be sent back home or given a new life. Maybe even testify against my employer. They whispered about a place called The Hotel."

Jordan moved away from Sloane, slowly striding across the dirt floor.

"But you lost one, didn't you, Marisol? You can't keep your eyes on them all the time. Probably because The Hotel isn't in Chicago, is it?"

A face flashed across her mind's eye. A young woman who'd heard too many threats from The Bishop and wouldn't wait at The Hotel for Marisol to get her back to Colombia. "Her name was Anna. Were you the one who hurt her?"

"I did more than that. Not until after she described who rescued her, though. Do you know what they call you?"

Marisol had spent weeks searching for Anna after she left the safety of The Hotel. She'd never found a trace and had foolishly hoped she'd managed to get home on her own.

"They call you The Dark Angel. *Ángel Oscuro*. She kept crying out for you to save her. If only she could see you now."

Jordan grabbed Marisol's hair and jerked her head back. Her neck screamed in pain but she didn't have the breath to give voice to it.

"Human trafficking." Sloane's voice cut through the air between them. "That's what this is all about. Sex trafficking. Where are you getting the girls?"

"People go missing all the time here in Colombia. The question," Jordan said in a quiet voice inches from Marisol's face. "Is where do they end up?"

Marisol's eyes began to roll. She prayed for unconsciousness, oblivion.

"Where is The Hotel, Marisol? Your little runaway couldn't tell us, but you can. Unless you want me to hang your guts from the rafters."

She released Marisol's head and it fell forward, her chin hitting hard against her chest. There was a moment of quiet anticipation. A heartbeat when the whole world stopped and Marisol thought her prayers might be answered, but they weren't. Her mind stayed aware and Jordan slammed the blunt end of the hook hard into her ribs on the right side. A sharp stab of pain erupted from the bones, but they held. For now.

Marisol heard the hook clatter to the floor and wondered whether her body could take this. She supposed it depended on what Jordan took out of the bag, but part of her was ambivalent. Whatever it was, it would hurt her and not kill her. She could hold on. For how long was the question. Perhaps another day. She only knew that she would not break right now.

She heard the crackle of arcing electricity a second before the prongs touched her abdomen and every muscle in her body seized.

CHAPTER TWENTY-TWO

"Tell me where it is, Marisol!"

Jordan was using her fists this time, secure inside fingerless boxing gloves. The padded knuckles kept her from splitting Marisol's face open. She pounded them in quick succession into Marisol's abdomen. Jordan wasn't a good enough boxer to know exactly where her kidneys were, but she was doing a good job of bruising Marisol from head to toe.

"Where is The Hotel?"

Marisol shook her head and the fists came again. Four or five shots to her ribs and then a lazy hook to her jaw. Her head jostled around like a worn out bobblehead doll. Her shoulders and neck ached so badly she wanted to scream. She kept her mouth shut and waited for the world to right itself again.

She squinted at the blur of blue in the corner of the room. The blur held perfectly still and gave Marisol an anchor point. As it came into focus, the red wave of Sloane's hair separated itself in hue from the now dirty sapphire of her dress. She stared unblinkingly at Marisol.

She let her mind empty as she stared into Sloane's eyes. The pain in her shoulders dulled. Her neck was only a pinprick of agony rather than a knife's blade. She tried to tell her face to smile, but her lips wouldn't comply. She tried to tell herself to wink, but she was too exhausted even for that. All she could do was stare, and she was surprised to find that Sloane did not look away.

Marisol knew when Jordan picked up the knife because Sloane's eyes widened. She turned to look at her tormentor. The overhead light shuddered as a large truck rumbled by on the dirt road outside. The vibration made it swing, the hypnotic movement of light flashing on the sharp blade.

Sloane screamed for her when the blade entered her bare bicep. It didn't cut deeply, just a fine slice. Marisol felt the hot trickle of blood on her cool skin. She focused on that rather than the pain.

"Who's your handler?"

Marisol's focus gave her new clarity. She heard the words of Sloane's scream rather than just the sound of it. Heard the plea for help that would never be answered. She let her eyes fall to the holster riding low on Jordan's hip. The hammer of Marisol's Colt glinted like the knife in swaying light. Jordan hadn't secured the thumb break. Apparently she wasn't worried about her weapon's security. She had no reason to worry about Marisol breaking free and Sloane had probably never even held a gun.

She tucked that thought away while Jordan cut again, an inch or so away from the first slice. This one was just a hair deeper and Marisol hissed a little as the blade went in. Sloane stopped screaming. Marisol could hear her crying.

"Where is it?"

The door wasn't far away. It would take only seconds to cross the room if her feet were free. A little longer if she couldn't cut the ropes around her ankles first. She would worry about that when she figured out how to get off the hook. She moved on to listening for more traffic on the road. She hadn't heard anything since the truck. It couldn't be a well-used road. She was probably on one of the estates dotting the hills around Bogota.

During the third cut, one of Jordan's minions slipped into the room while talking on a cell phone. He whispered into Jordan's ear and Marisol couldn't hear what he said, but she saw the door was still open. The shadows of feet on the other side moved away almost at once. She heard the faint sounds of cheering in the background and an echoing voice. A soccer match on TV.

The man left, pulling the door shut behind him. She couldn't tell if he'd secured the locks. Jordan dropped the knife onto the rickety, blood-splattered worktable beside her. Marisol knew Jordan would grab the cattle prod. She had time to close her eyes and let her head fall back before the electricity sent her into oblivion.

CHAPTER TWENTY-THREE

Sloane started shaking as Jordan left the room. She sat with her back against the wall hugging her knees hard to her chest. The metal wall jostled, filling her ears with a gentle rattle to accompany the buzz left by the cessation of Marisol's screams. Sloane knew she was losing control. Now her muscles were locked in place and her only movement was the involuntary tremor.

Her eyes were fixed on Marisol. At least she hoped they were fixed on Marisol and not Marisol's body. The bloody, broken husk that used to be Marisol. Sloane had worried she was dead since the last scream cut off with a wet gurgle and her head slumped onto her chest. Jordan prodded her a few times, perhaps hoping she was faking unconsciousness, but finally accepted that their interview was at an end. Since then, Marisol had hung from the hook like a side of beef, her arms stretched painfully.

Sloane watched her intently, following the slight, shallow movements of her tight gray T-shirt. It could be Marisol breathing or it could be a trick of Sloane's eyes. A desperate illusion she invented because she was begging her brain to see signs of life.

As Jordan left, she had dropped a bottle of water in Sloane's lap. She'd taunted Sloane about the tears that ran in a silent stream down her face. When Sloane had refused to engage her, Jordan had promised to return soon. The water sat untouched. Sloane was loathe to accept any offering from a sadist.

It was the thought of that evil that finally sent her to her feet. Marisol had been facing it alone. Whatever Marisol had been, whatever she was now, she certainly deserved a better death than this. They would both die, Sloane was sure of that now, but not yet. For now, Marisol had to be alive. She just had to be.

The first step was the hardest one. Once Sloane got it out of the way, she knew she could manage the short trip across to where Marisol was hanging. Several more steps and she lost her nerve, imagining what she would do if Marisol really was dead. She went back to collect the water bottle and took another deep breath. This trip took her all the way across the room, to stand in front of Marisol.

She heard wet, ragged breathing on the very edge of what was audible. It was enough to prove that Marisol was alive. Relief brought Sloane back to herself all at once, and her spine knitted into something solid again. Sliding the bandana from Marisol's pocket was easier this time. She cracked the top of the water bottle and poured a few drops onto it.

Marisol's knees had buckled, and she slumped so low that Sloane had to kneel to see her face. It was difficult in her tight dress, but she managed to bunch it around her waist and drop to her knees. Finding a place to begin on Marisol's dirt-streaked face was a much harder task. Her jaw looked the messiest spot, so Sloane touched the wet fabric there. The skin was streaked with blood, but not from attack. True to Jordan's word, she had avoided damaging Marisol's face, but she had grabbed her head often with blood-soaked hands. Sloane had always loved the slope of Marisol's regal jaw. This evidence of her ordeal did not diminish its beauty.

Marisol opened her eyes as Sloane wet the handkerchief again and pressed it to her face. She didn't move, even to take the weight off her tortured arms. Marisol's gaze met Sloane's as she stared back into those endless brown eyes. Her hand fell away from Marisol's jaw.

Sloane forced herself to look away, the stream of water wavering as she realized her hand was shaking. She set the bottle down and wrung out the cloth, delaying the time before she looked at Marisol.

When she did turn back, the eyes were still there. Still full of life and bravery. So full of emotion and strength. Sloane's lungs stopped at the sight. She swallowed hard and with the damp cloth reached toward Marisol's temple.

"Marisol…"

"No."

Sloane wasn't surprised that Marisol could read her mind. Worse still, her desire.

"Please." She swallowed hard and forced herself to look at the dried blood on Marisol's temple and not Marisol's penetrative look. "Please tell her what she wants to know."

"I can't do that."

"It's only one safe house." Sloane hated herself for saying the words. They tasted sour on her tongue, but she hated more the idea of Marisol's eyes never opening again. "There have to be others."

"There are a lot of people there, Brin. It's more than just a building."

There it was again. The nickname that made Sloane's heart feel lighter than air. Now that she'd heard it again, she didn't want to stop hearing it and that made her selfish in a way she'd never been before. Selfish enough to look back into those eyes and put voice to the thought that scared her the most.

"She'll kill you."

"Then I'll die. I'd rather die than let anyone hurt them again."

Regret, not fear, showed in her eyes. It was the regret that made Sloane so bitterly angry. She shot to her feet, towering over Marisol but standing so close their bodies nearly touched.

"Damn it, you need to look at the big picture!"

"Do you know what happens to them?"

Sloane didn't answer, which was answer enough. She'd put a few trafficked women on the witness stand, but she'd never really heard their stories. She'd only heard their testimony and she was starting to understand how different the two were. Marisol struggled to straighten her legs, getting some of her weight beneath her and finally relieving the strain in her shoulders. Once she was stable, she looked down into Sloane's eyes.

"They're taken from their homes. Some of them from the US, but most of The Bishop's come from around here. From Colombia where his money makes sure there are fewer questions asked. They're young, Brin. Very young."

Sloane hadn't tried any cases against human traffickers. She had closed down massage parlors and sent some pimps to jail, but those weren't men like this. It was a shock to realize just how small the fish she'd caught had been. Most of the women in those cases had been either convicted of petty crimes or, more often than she'd like to admit, deported. Frightened and abused women. She hadn't fought for them. She had let them go to whatever fate. What had they been through before? What had they been through after? Sloane shivered at the thought.

"Whatever you're thinking, it's nothing to what I've seen." A familiar ghost travelled across Marisol's eyes and she swallowed hard before she continued, "When there aren't any men willing to buy them anymore, the women are disposed of. If they cry too much or they refuse to do something, they're disposed of."

There was something in the wobble of Marisol's voice that suggested there was more to tell. She didn't give Sloane a chance to ask before she continued.

"I can't let Jordan, or worse, The Bishop, get them. Not a single one of them. If you'd seen what I've seen, you wouldn't tell me it isn't worth it."

The water bottle hit the floor and splashed against Sloane's legs. She didn't tell her hands to move, they did of their own accord, wrapping around Marisol's face. She held it up gently, cupping it reverently so they could look at each other. Sloane knew her eyes were wild with fear, but if that frightened Marisol now, all the better.

"There's no hope. We can't get out of here," Sloane hissed.

"You can. You will. If you do exactly what I say."

"I don't understand." She looked up at the rope tied so tightly around Marisol's wrists that her fingers were white and how she barely had enough slack to move her arms even now she was standing as upright as she could manage. She reached up to try pulling the rope free, but her fingers couldn't reach the hook. "I can't get you down. I'm not strong enough to lift you."

"I said *you* will get out. Now listen closely…"

"What? No!"

"Governor…"

"Stop it! No! I won't leave you!"

"God damn it, Brin!" Marisol's patience snapped, her face twisted in frustration. She continued in a whispered shout, "I did not go through all of this to watch you die! I have worked too hard for too many years to keep you alive to fail you now!"

Sloane's heart beat so loudly, she was sure Marisol could hear it. Blood pounded in her ears.

In a flash, Marisol's face was smooth and her voice silky. "Good girl. Now listen to me very carefully. There were only three men, as well as Hulk and Jordan here at the start. A car left during my last chat with Jordan."

Sloane's eyebrows came together as she tried to figure out how Marisol knew. She whipped her head around, certain she'd missed an open window all this time.

"I heard the engine and felt the vibration through the floor. I think two people went with it, that's why there's so little movement outside. I think it's just Jordan and two others now."

Straining to hear, Sloane just picked out a scuffing footstep through the wall.

"Jordan always comes in alone and closes the door without locking it. She's carrying a gun in a holster low on her hip. It isn't strapped in, so it'll be easy to get out. She's always worn it that way because she's sloppy and she likes a quick draw. Time to make her pay for it.

"When she comes in, I'll distract her. All you have to do is come over quickly and quietly. Grab the gun and run. Don't worry about Jordan. Don't shoot her unless you have to. Chances are the other two aren't paying attention by now, but they will if they hear the gun. Run past them and outside. If you're lucky, you can get out of here without firing a shot."

"I don't know if I…"

"You have to be quick. There's no way to know when the others will be back. They didn't take the van we came in. That hasn't moved since we got here. I know the sound of that engine. Get into the van and get the hell out of here. They left the keys in the ignition when we got here. I saw it when they were trying to pull me out. There's a purple rabbit's foot on a long chain hanging from the key. Clearly they aren't expecting us to try and escape. Drive west. Go to the nearest village and ask them to give you directions to Bogota. It isn't far. Go straight to our embassy and you'll be safe. If you don't have enough gas to get there, you can find a phone. I'll tell you the number of the embassy, okay?"

Marisol had the number memorized from her last trip and she called it out, slowly and quietly. Sloane nodded along, begging it to sink in. She repeated them when Marisol commanded her to, but got them wrong. Marisol told her the number again and the second time she repeated them back correctly. They wouldn't stay and Marisol's look said she knew the truth as well as Sloane.

"That's a good plan," Sloane said sarcastically.

"It'll work."

"There's just one problem."

"It'll work, Brin."

"I'm not a gun person." Her frayed nerves splintered and crumbled at her feet. "I've never even held a gun!"

"Shh!" Marisol hissed as she looked at the door. "Be quiet or you'll get us both killed."

She moderated her tone, but her words were still frantic. "I appreciate your confidence in me, but I have no idea how to shoot a gun."

"Point the open end at the bad guy and squeeze the trigger. You don't even have to hit them, just make them go for cover so you can run."

Everything in Marisol's face said she truly believed Sloane could do this. Sloane knew, beyond the shadow of a doubt, that she couldn't. She didn't argue the point. It scared her too much to think about how this would end. Instead, she picked up the water bottle.

She wiped the blood off Marisol's chin first, then the rest of her jaw. The room went quiet except for the gentle sounds of wet cloth against skin. She washed Marisol's split lip and tried to stop the tears from showing at the corner of her eyes.

"You can do this."

Sloane's voice was husky when she asked, "What will happen to you?"

"I'll keep her busy as long as I can. Until…Until you get away."

"Or until she kills you."

Marisol adjusted her weight, getting her feet beneath her more steadily. Her eyes were clear and they were fixed on Sloane's face. She nodded. Nothing extravagant, nothing showy, just the quick bob of her head in acceptance of her own imminent death.

"I need you to do something for me."

"Anything."

"When you get to the embassy…"

"When *we* get to the embassy."

"I need you to make a call." She looked to the door and dropped her voice even lower. Sloane could barely hear her over the unsaid words between them. "Call Dominique. She'll… know who to inform."

"She's your handler?" Marisol cringed as Sloane spoke the word aloud, but she nodded, her eyes back on Sloane. "So she's… not your girlfriend?"

"She was never my girlfriend."

The way she looked at Sloane said so much more than her words. For the first time in years, she wondered what would've happened if she'd gone to Mario's that night. Sloane brought the bottle to Marisol's newly cleaned lips. She tilted her head back and Sloane poured the water in a thin stream. Marisol drank greedily and Sloane watched her long, lean neck bob as she swallowed. They moved at the same time, Sloane removing the bottle and Marisol lowering her head.

Sloane reached up and dabbed the water away from Marisol's lips. "Why are you doing this?"

Marisol blinked slowly and then looked into Sloane's eyes. Something shifted in Marisol. She was beyond arguing. Beyond fighting. Beyond hiding. She was raw.

"Because I love you." There was a moment of quiet. "I've loved you since the moment I met you in that yuppie bar all those years ago. It wasn't the sex. It was you. I couldn't get enough of you. I knew that guy had told you who I was when you didn't turn up at the bar after our day on court. But I followed your career and I loved you even more. When you took down all the vermin like me in Chicago. If my… If my life had been different, maybe…"

Marisol stopped and looked away. Every muscle in Sloane's body was frozen in place until Marisol spoke again.

"The first time I saved your life it was an accident. I wanted to see you again, after the coffee shop and the date you didn't show for. And again, after the deposition where you acted like you'd never met me. I went to your press conference when you pressed charges against the cop who'd killed the little Black boy playing with a toy gun. I left as you were taking questions from the press. There were a bunch of white supremacists outside, trying to ambush you on the way to your car in the alley. They were easy to take out. Idiots.

"I watched from behind a dumpster as you got safely into your car and drove away. My heart split in two that day. Half drove away with you in that sedan. The other half kept me alive only enough to protect the half I sent with you. You were the only thing in my life worth living for. You are the only thing worth dying for. I love you, Brin. I always have."

Sloane kept herself perfectly still and silent until Marisol ran out of words. She hung there, acting as though it was acceptable to declare undying love and her intention to die in the same breath and then say nothing more.

Just as suddenly as Marisol had declared her love, Sloane decided her own course. She had denied her feelings for too long. She should've given in years ago. She should've kissed Marisol in the coffee shop. Should've followed her after the deposition. She should've slapped that tequila out of her hand on the Drake Hotel's balcony. Now, in the quiet horror of this place, she would finally give in to her desire.

Sloane threw herself at Marisol, pressing their lips together with wild, joyous desperation. She kissed Marisol and tasted blood and felt her whole life come together as it never had before. Marisol kissed back with everything she had, even with her pain and her weakness and her hands bound over her head. They lost themselves in each other.

With one hand, Sloane held Marisol's face close, with the other she pulled their whole bodies flush, dragging Marisol to her. The hook over their heads rattled as Marisol tried to wrap Sloane in her arms but was thwarted by the bindings.

The heat of Marisol's breath in Sloane's mouth was intoxicating. It gripped her and drove her wild. She pulled Marisol's face closer. Sloane moaned into her mouth, her stomach lurching pleasantly as her body electrified. Her fingers slid into the damp hair at the back of Marisol's neck. She whimpered as they kissed harder, the sound soft in Sloane's ears.

Their mouths and bodies fit as closely as puzzle pieces. The closer they got, the more danger Sloane felt of forgetting where they were. Forgetting who was in the next room. Forgetting the taste of blood on her tongue where she was being too rough with her damaged partner.

She teetered on the edge of forgetting for a long time, reveling in Marisol's kisses and the feel of her body. Her mind screamed for her to be sensible, but logic drowned in the singing of her flesh. Slowly, agonizingly, she ended the kiss, separating their bodies first and then their lips. Marisol appeared just as reluctant to break the kiss.

Sloane was slow to open her eyes. She knew what she would see. Marisol's flashing brown eyes soaking in lust, as were her own. When her lids fluttered open, however, she saw something completely unexpected. Fear in Marisol's eyes. A panicked, animal fear that had not appeared once in all the beatings. She wasn't looking at Sloane. She was looking over her shoulder.

Before she could turn. Before she could think. Before she could do anything a searing pain exploded on Sloane's scalp. The hair on the back of her head lifted in a violent yank and her head snapped back. Cold fingers wrapped around her throat, and blackness crept into the edges of her vision as she fought to breathe.

"Looks like I've found your weakness at last, Marisol."

Sloane saw a brief flash of Jordan's hateful face before it was gone. Then Marisol's face was gone, too. With a single, violent yank Jordan sent her flying across the room.

Sloane threw up her arms instinctively, but that only made matters worse. Her ribs caught against one of the roof pillars. Pain erupted up her side and through her chest, forcing the air from her body. She spun a few degrees in midair, then crashed to the ground in a heap.

She heard a scream of frustrated anger, but it couldn't be hers. It was a primal, agonized scream that exploded into the stillness the instant before her shoulder smashed into the ground, followed by the sharp smack from the crown of her head. She didn't have breath to scream. Stars erupted in her vision as she gasped for air. The loose dirt of the floor flew into her nostrils and coated her dry mouth. She coughed and the sound was choked.

She didn't lose consciousness, but the world swam sickeningly. Marisol's scream filled her mind. Then the cold fingers were back around her throat. Her temple pulsed as the blood built pressure against her skin. She tried to beg for help, but her mind could not form the words and her lungs didn't have the air to make them.

In the dim recesses of her mind, she understood what was happening. She saw Jordan's face hovering over her. She felt the woman's free arm wrench hers over her head at an angle that could have broken it. She felt her clothing move as the blackness hovering on the edges of her vision crept slowly toward the center.

Her flailing mind brought up the image of Dominique Levy, the gentle, thoughtful woman she had seen last at her Inaugural Ball. The one who had told her that one day she might find a hidden depth to Marisol. The one who apparently knew those depths better than anyone. She must remember to tell Dominique she was right about Marisol.

CHAPTER TWENTY-FOUR

Marisol had entered a perfect nightmare. She had been in the heights of ecstasy. A decade's worth of hopeless fantasies had suddenly come true. Sloane's body had been pressed against hers. They were kissing and Marisol had forgotten a kiss could be so divine. Could make her believe in a god out there in the void.

Then she had opened her eyes and Jordan's smug, malevolent face was inches away. Everything she had worked so hard to keep hidden from her kidnapper was hellishly displayed in Jordan's smile of pure, delighted evil, revealing the horrors that were to come. Now she was trapped, hanging from this hook like a slab of useless meat, about to watch Jordan defile the most beautiful thing the universe had ever created.

Marisol couldn't remember the last time she had felt this kind of wild, impotent fury. She had fought the sense of helplessness all her life. If she had ever stopped to consider her choices, every single one of them from the time she was a little girl staring into her dead mother's eyes until this day had been to avoid being helpless. Yet here she was, in the most important moment of her life, feet tied, hands bound over her head. She would never be able to get her body high enough to unhook them.

In an act of pure self-hatred, Marisol let herself look at the struggle across the room. Jordan was laughing now. A high-pitched victorious wheeze. She'd released Sloane's throat, but the Governor's lips were still tinged blue and her face was a vivid shade of purple. Her head wobbled drunkenly and her eyes were vague as they spun.

With one hand she pinned Sloane's wrists to the floor above her head. The other roughly hiked up Sloane's tight skirt, ripping a seam. She pressed her body between Sloane's knees and there was no doubt as to her intention.

The sight enraged Marisol and she screamed again, the force of her rage propelling her body forward as far as the hook permitted. Even through her blind fury, she felt the easy glide of rope along metal and analyzed it. Perhaps her bonds were not as securely attached to the hook as she thought. She screamed again, this time more to cover the sounds of her movement than out of blind panic. The nylon rope shifted again.

Sloane, who had a cut high on her forehead that bled freely down her dust-streaked cheek, seemed to regain a sliver of her senses. Jordan's hand snaked under the tightly bunched dress, but Sloane struggled enough that Jordan had to abandon her attempts to get beneath her clothing.

Something irrevocable inside Marisol snapped. As Jordan's hand wrapped around Sloane's throat again, the Governor opened her mouth in a silent, gurgling scream. It was a sound Marisol knew all too well. Sloane's eyes, clearer than before, slid from Jordan's face, across the room to land on Marisol. There was desperation in them. Pleading.

Marisol's vision went red with fury. She couldn't let it happen. She would not let another woman she loved be taken from her like this. Watching someone else choke the life out of the most important person to her. Sloane's bare foot began to shake.

A roar originated in her very core and Marisol spewed it from her mouth like venom. At the same moment she jumped as high as she could with what little leverage the ground could provide her stretched toes. Her plan was thin. Ridiculously thin. It would crumble in an instant at the slightest wrong touch, but it was her only hope and she had to act.

The rope binding her wrists came free of the hook. She grabbed with numb hands at the long, metal stick of the hook and somehow managed to hold on. She gripped it tightly, her hands in agony from the strain, but it didn't matter. She was free of the hook, but she had more work to do.

Jordan adjusted her grip and Sloane's shouting finally had enough room to give voice. "No! No! No!"

Jordan laughed and scooted her knees higher beneath her. She released Sloane's hands, but Sloane's attempts to retaliate were worthless. Even as Jordan's free hand went back to pulling Sloane's dress up, the hand around her throat clamped down, cutting off her cries.

Marisol forced herself to focus on her task. Her plan stood on a knife's edge now, and she needed to be very careful. Unfortunately, her bloodless hands were already sliding down the smooth surface of the hook and she needed to be higher to clear the hooked end when she let go. Kicking her powerful legs through the air beneath her, Marisol jumped again, gripping the hook arm a little higher than before. She blocked out Jordan's laughter, thankful only that her distraction afforded Marisol time. She was close now. Almost there, but her hands were agony after being hung by them for so long and she was losing her grip.

In an instant, Marisol registered both that she was not high enough on the hook and that she was at the limit of her strength. Her grip was failing and she was going to fall. Her bonds would slide back down the metal arm and she would be trapped again.

Summoning all her remaining strength in one final, monumental effort, Marisol swung her legs, kicked and jumped. Only this time, when she let go of the hook, she swung the rope back, away from her bindings. She felt the very tip of the hook scrape along the surface of the rope. It stuttered, caught, couldn't find purchase, and finally, miraculously, swung free.

Marisol fell in a heap to the ground. Her ankle twisted and her face smacked hard into the packed dirt, but she was free. Her body begged to remain on the floor. Every injury it had received since she came crashing through an air vent in Sloane's luxury apartment building in Chicago ached and held her fast to the ground. But she was Marisol Soltero, The Queen of Humboldt, and she dragged herself to her feet.

She stood, took a deep breath, and charged. Her movements were jerky, shuffling, and distinctly ungraceful because of her tied ankles, but she was aimed at Jordan and she was gaining speed. She didn't look at Sloane. She couldn't. If she saw the blackening features or the slow, inevitable drooping of her limbs, Marisol would crumble. Instead she put all of her effort into her awkward run. The ropes cut into her right ankle where the leg of her leather pants had ridden up her calf, and her charge gained a hopping skip as she neared her target.

Just when Marisol thought she could take her tormentor by surprise, Jordan's head snapped up. She saw Marisol coming and released Sloane's neck, twisting to meet the onrushing attack. It was too late. Another two skipping steps and Marisol lowered her body, ramming her shoulder directly into Jordan's chest as she stood to meet the charge.

At the moment of impact, Marisol's world blinked out in pain. It came back almost immediately, but the pain redoubled when they slammed together into the floor. Marisol's shoulder wrenched. Her back slammed so hard into the floor that all the breath was knocked from her lungs.

Jordan and Marisol tumbled over each other, the momentum of the collision rolling them across the room in a jumble of flailing limbs and curses in two languages. Most unfortunately, Jordan landed on top. Her knee dug into Marisol's already brutalized side as she struggled to her feet. With stoic inevitability, Marisol watched Jordan stand. Instinctively she knew the fight was over. Her efforts were Herculean, but they were not enough.

As she rolled onto her back, Marisol knew she didn't have the strength to get back up. She had fought her body for every last particle of strength and now there was truly nothing left. She barely had the strength to breathe.

Marisol watched helplessly as Jordan pulled herself up to her full height. She loomed over Marisol, her expression full of mingled hatred and glee. Her hand reached toward the holster on her hip. Marisol swallowed hard and waited for the end of her pain.

She had given everything she had to this world and it had only taken, giving nothing to her in return. Nothing but a perfect weekend and a single kiss. All the bad she had done and the little bit of good had been worth it for that one, perfect kiss. She stopped the thought of what would happen to Sloane after she was dead. It appeared on the horizon of her thoughts and she turned away from it. Her last memory would be that Brin had kissed her. She had learned everything of who Marisol was and she had kissed her anyway. It had been worth living for. It was certainly worth dying for.

Two gunshots in quick succession exploded into the night. Just as quickly two roses bloomed on Jordan's chest, all shining scarlet and twisted petals. Her mouth drooped from a smirk into a straight, neutral line. Her eyes dimmed and she spat a mouthful of blood into the dusty air. She stood still as a statue for a single moment, then crumpled into a heap at Marisol's feet.

Her fall revealed Sloane standing a few feet away. She was shaking like a leaf, her finger still wrapped around the trigger of Marisol's shining Colt. Her eyes were wild with panic.

A sudden silence filled the room and Marisol realized she'd heard the muffled roar of a crowd and the impassioned bark of sports announcers until that moment. She lay still, waiting for the television sounds to start again, but instead she heard the shuffling of booted feet. She scrambled to her knees with difficulty, forced to push herself upright on her sore elbow and bruised shoulder.

"Boss?"

The man's voice, calling through the door, was as good a cover as Marisol could hope to have. She shuffled awkwardly to Jordan's feet, using her bound hands to search the tops of her boots. Jordan had always carried a boot knife. She'd enjoyed whipping out the blade dramatically and, though Marisol had rolled her eyes at the time, she was relieved now to find Jordan had continued the habit.

"Hey," the man called again, an edge of annoyance cutting through his words. "You kill 'em? I thought I heard gunshots."

The ropes around her wrists allowed her just enough play to position the knife but sawing through them was a challenge. Fortunately, Jordan kept her knife sharp and Marisol was able to slice through the coils quickly. She had her right hand free of the ropes when she heard the familiar sound of screeching hinges as the heavy door began to open.

Marisol leapt forward, calculating the angle of her movement even as she performed it. As she dove over Jordan's corpse she tucked her shoulder and rolled. Her feet came to the ground again, she dug the toes of her boots into the earth. She propelled her body as far away from Sloane as she could and landed on her knees directly across from the door.

The first guy was one of those who had strung her up on the hook. One step into the room and Marisol dropped him, his machete spinning across the floor. Jordan's boot knife protruded from the base of his throat and he gurgled as he fell. Throwing the knife was agony on her abused shoulder. Even she was surprised at the accuracy of her throw with her recently freed hand. Blood was still working its way to her fingertips and the pins and needles made it difficult to use them.

Rather than attempt to stand, Marisol tucked her arms across her chest and rolled toward the discarded machete. Wielding a two-handed weapon was a risk given the ropes still hanging from her left hand, but her opponent wasn't much of a threat. He clearly thought he was entering the room to help dispose of Marisol and Sloane's corpses, and so he was unprepared for attack. Marisol hacked at his knee and he roared in pain, crumbling in front of her. She silenced him quickly, his hand never touching the rifle slung across his shoulder. Rolling back to the first man, she checked to see he was no longer a threat before turning her attention to Sloane.

She hadn't moved. She still stared wide-eyed at Jordan's body, the gun gripped in her hands.

"Brin?"

Marisol kept her voice quiet, but maybe she was too quiet. Sloane stood silently, the gun quaking in a thousand directions.

"Put the gun down." Sloane didn't move her arm, only her eyes moved, spreading even wider and darting around. Marisol put the slightest edge to her voice. "Brin, look at me."

It was a calculated risk, Marisol knew. People holding guns, particularly those new to the sensation, tended to move the weapon to wherever their eyes went. True to form, Sloane whipped her gaze around to fix on Marisol and she brought the barrel of the gun with her. She told herself that she trusted Sabrina Sloane. That she was a strong woman who could handle this moment. Still, it was more than exhaustion that made Marisol shift with slow, ponderous movements as she shuffled forward on her knees.

Sloane looked away from her, focusing back on Jordan's body, and the gun went with her gaze. With almost the same effort it took to get herself off the hook, Marisol climbed to her feet. She could already see the red marks of Jordan's fingers coming to life on Sloane's gorgeous neck. She gritted her teeth against the image and shuffled to her side.

"I shot her."

The voice did not sound like Sloane's. If Marisol hadn't seen her lips move, she wouldn't have believed the source.

"It's okay."

Sloane whipped her eyes up. Had Marisol thought they were wild before? Now they were feral. Crazed. Deranged. She waved the gun around as she spoke, the barrel cutting a warm trail through the air so close to Marisol's face that she nearly flinched away.

"Okay? How is this okay? This is not okay! A woman is dead! *I killed her!*"

"Brin." Her voice was firm but patient. Finally, Sloane's eyes cleared a fraction and she really looked at Marisol for the first time. "It's okay, baby."

The tears came like lighting out of a clear blue sky. One moment Sloane's eyes were dry, the next she was weeping uncontrollably. She dropped the gun. It rattled on the floor and tumbled until it rested, butt up against Jordan's boot. Sloane threw her arms around Marisol, sobbing into her neck and mumbling incoherently. Marisol hugged her back with what little strength she possessed, tucking her chin against Sloane's shoulder.

She could have spent the rest of her life like this with Sloane's warm, solid presence pressed against her body. The feel of her lips and her nose pressed into the soft flesh of her neck. The grip of needy fingers on her damp T-shirt. There had been precious few genuinely good moments in Marisol's life. Any that she had were always tinged with bad, and this was no exception. Still, she reveled in it for the mere fact that they were both alive for the time being.

Her exhaustion was too much in the end and she couldn't keep her feet. She managed it gracefully until she hit her knees, but she fell the rest of the way to her side. Sloane was on her in a heartbeat, yanking at the ropes around her wrist. Marisol bit off her yelp of pain as the ropes yielded quickly. The moment her hands were free, Sloane gripped them hard in her own, pulling them in a knot to rest against her chest. She leaned forward in a flash of movement and pressed Marisol into another searing kiss.

Shock as much as lust accounted for Marisol's immediate response, but she did not have time to fall into the kiss. As soon as it began, Sloane broke the contact and leapt to her feet. If nothing else, Marisol was able to take the brief kiss as proof that their first was not inspired by the proximity of death.

Sloane grabbed the machete and brought it back to Marisol. She knelt at Marisol's feet, positioning the machete, which trembled wildly along with every other inch of her body, to chop down through the ropes. In her current state, it was far more likely that she would chop off both Marisol's feet.

"I'll do that."

Sloane scowled and sawed through the ropes. The blade was sharp and as soon as the job was done, Sloane dropped the machete. Marisol considered taking it herself, but instead she snatched up her beloved Colt.

They heard tires crunching outside and Marisol was on her feet. She grabbed Sloane's hand and they rushed headlong toward the door and freedom.

Bright white light cut through the breaks in the wall as the car turned toward their building, but by then the two fugitives were on their way through the outer room. A boxy TV sat precariously on a wooden crate, a soccer game flashing silently to the empty room. Marisol didn't stop to check for weapons. Their time was running out and she had to retrace the steps she'd taken with a bag over her head hours ago.

They burst out of the building, Sloane running barefoot with surprising agility. Just as Marisol suspected, the van still sat in front with the cargo doors facing the entrance. Sloane didn't need direction, she dropped Marisol's hand and sprinted to the passenger's door.

As Marisol wrenched the driver's door open and slipped into the seat, she turned toward the car skidding to a halt at the far corner of the building. Hulk jumped out before the tires stopped, locking his eyes on Marisol as she turned the van's key. The engine roared, covering his shout. The back passenger door of Hulk's car opened and Marisol saw the face she had been dreading.

Judging by his silver hair, The Bishop was in his late fifties. His broad, flat face had a thin mustache and a look of cold fury. He was not screaming in rage like Hulk. He wasn't barking instructions or pointing. He simply stared into Marisol's eyes as she stared back and in them she saw her own death. She became aware of Sloane, hidden by the night shadows behind her and determined that this evil man would not see her face.

The man's lip twisted in a snarl and Marisol slammed her foot into the gas pedal. She heard a spray of dirt and rocks behind them as the van sped off into the inky night.

CHAPTER TWENTY-FIVE

"Hey Gray."

"Marisol, you wanna tell me what the hell's going on?"

"Who do we know in Bogota?"

"No one friendly."

"Didn't think so."

The conversation lagged as they both listened to the watery crackle of static on the line. Marisol wasn't surprised by the bad connection. She stood behind the counter of a run-down service station on the edge of nowhere. She leaned to get a view out the side door she had banged on a few minutes ago, waking the proprietor and his wife. Morning was rapidly approaching, the sun spilling pale light over the sleepy village. She couldn't see the van hidden in the low scrub, and that made her a fraction more comfortable.

The proprietor adjusted his seat, picking at his teeth with a worn toothpick and studiously ignoring her presence. People in this area had become very used to pretending they didn't see things. Pretending they didn't hear things.

A girl of maybe four or five sat on the floor of the shop, playing with a doll. She was the only clean thing in the place and her father was keeping a protective eye on her though he feigned indifference well. His concern and his watchfulness made Marisol trust him in a way she hadn't before.

"Glad you're alive, boss."

"Don't crack the champagne yet. I'm a long way from safe."

"Word is Governor Sloane was involved in some sort of situation last night, but the cops are keeping everything real quiet." He paused, probably waiting for her to comment. When she didn't offer one, he took a more direct route. "You wouldn't know nothing about that, would you?"

Marisol thought it wise to redirect the conversation. "Do you have eyes on Dominique?"

There was a split second of silence on the line and Marisol's heart stopped and started a dozen times during that second. What if Jordan had figured out Dominique's importance once she'd eliminated Sloane as a potential handler?

"Funny you should mention it," he said. "She stopped by last night looking for you."

"Where is she now?"

"Upstairs in your place. Says it feels like a hotel. Maybe you oughta finish moving in."

"Send her up some breakfast and ask her to wait for me."

There was an impatient sneer in Gray's voice when he replied, "She put in an order last night. Seems to think your place comes with room service."

Marisol smiled despite herself. Her mind at ease about Dominique's safety, she turned back to securing her own. "How soon can you get down here?"

"Let me round up some boys and…"

"No. No boys. Come alone and come quiet."

"Extraction?"

"Yeah."

"Marisol, I think we should have backup. That's hostile territory."

"I said no."

A short, plump woman with a kind smile and one eye glazed with cataract despite her young age emerged from the back of the store.

"Keep your cell on you. I'll call in two hours and you better be in the air by then."

He said something else, but she dropped the phone back into the cradle. The little woman stalked between the shelves with efficient if ungraceful movements, grabbing items and dropping them into a net bag. The man behind the counter split his wary gaze between his wife and daughter, his shoulders pinching in concern.

Marisol bent and untied her right boot. Each movement sent a cascade of pain through her body, but it was duller now. Aches more than pains really. Peeling the boot off, she slid out the false bottom and retrieved the stash of bills concealed inside. She held out the wad to the woman when she approached, holding out the bag to Marisol.

Looking concernedly at Marisol's face she tried to wave it off. Her husband flinched but said nothing. Marisol insisted, pressing the money with a few words of thanks into the woman's pillow-soft palm. She turned, but the woman grabbed her arm and held up her forefinger before slipping behind the counter. Marisol caught the roll of the man's eyes, but his wife missed it.

After some rummaging, she popped up with a jar in her hand. It looked like some kind of paste, dark green and speckled with something brown. She tried to explain to Marisol what it was, but her words were a mixture of Spanish and an indigenous dialect. Marisol guessed she was at least part Muisca, the tribe most common in this part of Colombia, but she couldn't be sure. All she understood was that this paste would help her wounds. She thought the woman said something about reducing swelling, but it was hard to tell.

Marisol tucked the jar into the pocket of her leather jacket and with another warm round of appreciation to the store owners, picked up the net bag and a can of gasoline, then edged to the door. She was keenly aware of how long she had been in the building and didn't want to bring these people harm or be caught herself. Not when she and Sloane were this close to freedom.

The village boasted little modern convenience, so the residents would most likely be up with the sun. She strolled along the road, close to the tree line, and walked past the van's hiding spot without breaking stride. She felt the store owner's eyes on her back and, though she was grateful, she couldn't rely on him to keep her secrets if danger rolled down on his family. Eventually someone would ask about two American women in a van. If he never saw Sloane or the van, they might leave him alone.

Several hundred yards past the van, Marisol turned off the road into the cover of scrub. All too aware of the potential for prying eyes watching from the hills, she ducked behind a low tree. She waited for a long moment, listening for pursuing footsteps. Hearing nothing, she picked her way back under the cover of vegetation. It was a longer, rougher route and Marisol felt every inch of it in her tortured body, but she kept walking at a half-crouch.

Marisol slipped inside the driver's door, dropping the supplies on the empty passenger seat. As she fired the engine into life, Sloane came crawling up from the back, trying to slip into the front with her. Marisol held out a restraining hand, keeping her eyes fixed on the dirty windshield. If anyone was watching she didn't want them to see her respond.

"Stay down and out of sight."

"But it's…"

"Someone may be watching," She said to the dashboard, her lips barely moving. "I don't think they saw you back at the compound. I don't want them to see you now."

"They knew I was there. Where would they think I've gone?"

"To hell for all I care. I'm not giving them proof. Besides, there's every chance Jordan didn't tell anyone she'd made the mistake of kidnapping a United States Governor and transporting her out of the country."

Sloane may have wanted to argue the point further, but Marisol threw the van into gear and rolled out onto the main road. When she dropped a pair of simple, woven sandals on the floor Sloane took them with her back into the cargo space while Marisol drove.

For hours she wove her way through one small, mountain community to another. If she headed straight to Bogota, they'd track her down immediately. The enemy would expect a quick sprint for safety and they knew the area far better than she did. Instead of doing the expected, she would find a place to hide out until Gray could arrive. They would make their way to the city under cover of night.

When the sun was directly overhead and the village they entered looked like it was deep in the grip of siesta, Marisol slowed the van and scanned the buildings. Like many communities here in the Eastern Hills, there were a good number of ramshackle buildings that may or may not be occupied. She spotted her target near the far end of town.

She picked up speed again as she passed the building and continued out into the countryside and she spotted an appropriate stand of trees. She wedged the vehicle between them and left the keys in the ignition, sparing a moment to refill the gas tank in case a quick getaway was necessary. She heard Sloane opening the rear door as she collected the shopping bag and her Colt. Tucking her gun into the band of her pants, she put her lips close to Sloane's ear and whispered to her to follow, quickly and quietly.

The hike back to town was arduous if uneventful. Marisol had no difficulty locating the building with its spacious shed out back. Slipping inside, she saw that it had actually been a machine shop before it was abandoned, which accounted for its size. It was almost as large as the house, though, unlike the house, the shed's roof was intact.

Making her way to the back of the shop, Marisol found a room tucked away in the corner of the building. Like everything else, it was covered in a thick layer of dust. The mattress on the floor looked clean enough and did not appear to harbor any mice, but she flipped it to be certain and nothing scurried out. It fell with a flop, sending a cloud of dust into the air.

Near the mattress was an old couch covered in a dusty sheet, as was the rest of the sparse furniture. She whipped the sheet off quickly enough that most of the dust fell on the ground rather than the couch and tossed it aside. It fluttered down to rest, clean side up, on the mattress. The day was warm enough, even here in the mountains, that she doubted they would need cover while they slept. She poked at the cushions of the couch but didn't feel anything move.

As soon as the couch was uncovered, Sloane collapsed onto it. Sweat stained the high neckline of her dress and down the zipper on its back. She looked exhausted, but Marisol was pleased to see she was not cracking. Killing for the first time wasn't easy, particularly for someone like Brin, but it didn't seem to have hit her yet. This exhaustion was physical, not emotional.

Marisol settled down next to her and unpacked the bag. The woman had managed to fit a surprising number of useful supplies into it. On top was a pair of aluminum trays with paper lids, the heat was long gone from them, but the smell of hearty beans and pungent rice made her mouth water. She set the trays aside for now, but they would get her full attention soon enough.

Next out of the bag were several bottles of water, some fresh fruit she didn't take the time to identify, packs of bandages and a rattling bottle she sincerely hoped held painkillers. She could've wished for a bottle of tequila and maybe even a toothbrush, but she would take what she could get. She discarded everything in favor of what she needed most—a burner cell phone still held in its bubble packaging.

"Eat something," Marisol said, attacking the phone packaging.

Sloane snatched it from her and set it on the floor, putting herself between it and Marisol. She tore open the wrapping on a pack of bandages and glared at her companion. "I'm cleaning you up, then we can eat."

Marisol made a lunge for the phone, but Sloane moved with her. Their bodies nearly collided before Marisol stopped. She scowled, looking into Sloane's eyes. It was a look that had cowed grown men, but it had no effect on Sloane. She stared back, still determined, still calm.

"I have to make a call first."

"After I clean you up."

It wasn't a suggestion or a compromise. It was the closest thing to an order Marisol had heard in fifteen years. Her eyebrow shot up of its own accord. She considered a sarcastic reply, but the words died on her tongue. Considering nearly every inch of her body varied between sore and downright agony, she let the order stand. She sat back against the couch and pulled the bottle of green paste from her jacket pocket, handing it to Sloane.

"What's this?"

Marisol shook a couple pills from the bottle and washed them down with lukewarm water. "Medicine."

"What kind?"

Marisol shrugged and Sloane snatched the bottle from her, using it to wash her hands before unscrewing the jar's lid. The scent hit her immediately, cool and grassy with the bite of peppers and an herbaceous earthiness. The aroma alone made her relax. Sloane dipped two fingers into the jar, pulling up a scoop of paste and testing its texture between her fingers.

"It's like sand," she said, concern cutting lines into her weary face. "It might hurt when I rub it in."

"I'll be fine."

Sloane reached out, smearing the paste onto Marisol's right cheek. It did feel like sand at first and her skin, stretched and puffy with bruising, protested. After a moment of contact, however, the paste cooled the angry sting and even the aching soon faded. Marisol closed her eyes and couldn't hold back a sigh.

"Does it hurt? I can stop."

"No," Marisol replied, her muscles turning to jelly. "It's good. Don't stop."

Sloane's touch was gentle as it spread the miracle salve over her cheek and jaw. As she massaged the paste in, her fingers on Marisol's skin brought back heat. The pain leaked away and

Marisol turned her entire focus to Sloane's touch. Her tenderness and her proximity lit a fire throughout Marisol's body, far from where their skin met. She moved down Marisol's neck, dipping below her shirt collar following a line of rope burn.

Marisol shrugged out of her jacket, draping it across the back of the couch, and Sloane tended to the cuts on her arm.

When she felt the tail of her shirt lift, Marisol's eyes flew open. Sloane pushed the T-shirt up, revealing a set of bruises across her abdomen that shocked and sickened Marisol. It was one thing to know the signs of her torture existed, it was another entirely to see them marking her own skin. Sloane's focus was entirely on the jar of paste, scooping up another heap.

Though she had time to prepare, Marisol's abs still clenched involuntarily at the press of Sloane's fingers against her skin. She looked up anxiously, but Marisol nodded and she went back to work. She couldn't very well explain that it wasn't pain that had caused the reaction, but rather the vision of Sloane rubbing her stomach. She closed her eyes again, letting the rippling chill from the paste distract her from the fire in her belly. She nearly moaned when Sloane's fingertips brushed against the waistband of her leather pants.

"Where else?"

Marisol, lost in thoughts of Sabrina Sloane's fingers and her waistband, croaked, "What?"

"Where else are you hurting?" There was an edge of strain to Sloane's voice. "Didn't she...um, your back?"

"Right. Yeah."

Marisol turned around, leaning over the arm of the couch, and pulled her T-shirt up around her neck. It caught on her bra for a moment, then gave way and settled against her shoulders. This time Marisol heard Sloane's quiet hiss, and she knew Jordan's fun with a belt and a length of discarded rope had left behind something unpleasant. She felt Sloane slide forward on the cushions and a moment later her skin was on Marisol's again. Either the effect of the paste was wearing off, or Marisol was having a harder time ignoring Sloane's touch. The sensation was far less clinical than it should have been.

While coating her upper back, Sloane asked in a small voice, "Did you really want to have drinks with me? When you asked me out at the coffee shop?"

"Of course I did. That's why I asked."

"So I wasn't some assignment from the NSA?"

"An assignment?"

Sloane's fingers stilled, resting lightly against her spine. Marisol held the sensation, willing the memory to last a lifetime.

Finally, Sloane continued, "Did the NSA ask you to get close to me? Did you save my life under orders?"

Marisol turned, but couldn't see Sloane's face over her shoulder. All she could see was the slope of her thigh and the long line of her outstretched arm. Even this shuttered glimpse, added to the doubt in her voice, was enough to show Marisol how worried she was. How hopeful.

"I didn't know who you were that day, Brin." Her own hope had evaporated with the cop who'd glared at her across the courthouse steps and then whispered to Sloane. That had sent Marisol home alone that night. "Not any more than you knew who I was."

"And after?"

Marisol turned back around, letting her head fall against her forearms resting on the couch. "No one in Washington knows how I feel about you. If they did, I'd be worthless to them."

Sloane's hand moved again, smearing the paste in a thin streak down Marisol's spine. "Why?"

"Because I'd have something that could be used against me." She swallowed hard, planning her next words carefully to protect her exposed heart. "I'm valuable because I don't care about anything."

"You care about the women you save."

Sloane said it so matter-of-factly, so plainly, that Marisol's heart raced. Two days ago she had been convinced Marisol was the lowest scum on earth. Now she was defending Marisol's goodness against her own denials.

"And *they* use that against *me*. They're not about to fall on their own sword."

Sloane spread paste down Marisol's back, nearing the waistband of her jeans again. Her hand detoured along her side and Marisol ached for her to keep it here. To pull Marisol close and hold her. She knew it was the wrong time and the wrong place to crave Sloane's touch, but the more of it she got, the more she wanted.

"Dominique knows," Sloane said after a long silence.

"Why do you say that?"

"I talked to her once. After I left you on the balcony at my Inaugural Ball. I ran into her in the bathroom."

Sloane slid the jar's lid back into place. Marisol thought of that night. How she'd had too much tequila and talked too much. How Dominique had watched her while the limo took them home. Had Marisol indulged less that night, she might've suspected Dominique's gaze had held meaning, but then if she'd indulged less she'd never have had the nerve to talk to Sloane in the first place.

"That explains a lot," Marisol replied with a laugh. "She's very perceptive."

"Do you think she told the people in Washington?"

"Absolutely. She's a loyal friend, but she's devoted to them."

"Why?"

Marisol pulled her shirt down and turned back to Sloane. "I've been trying to figure that out for a long time."

"But you still trust her?"

Marisol nodded, keeping her eyes locked on Sloane. She hadn't been this close to her in so long, she wanted to feel it. To take in her warmth and her electricity. After so long in the shadows, it was strange to be out in the open like this. To let Sloane see her for what she was. She forced herself to stay here, to enjoy this time.

Sloane held out the jar, letting Marisol take it from her hands. "I think that's everything."

Marisol knew it was wishful thinking, but she imagined she heard a reluctance in Sloane's voice.

CHAPTER TWENTY-SIX

Sloane came awake all at once, curled up on the couch, her head on one arm and her knees tucked to her chest. A leather jacket was draped across her, keeping out the chill of the evening air that touched her cheeks. She couldn't remember where she was or how she'd gotten there. She recognized the jacket and the smell at the collar—sweat and a musky cologne—was comfortingly familiar.

Fighting to understand, she struggled to find what had woken her. There had been a sound, a horrible sound. It all came flooding back then. The sound had been in her dream. The sound of Jordan's body falling to the ground after she'd shot her. She swallowed hard as she pushed herself upright, expecting panic to overwhelm her at any moment.

To her great surprise, she was calm. Sloane had never thought herself capable of taking another's life. She thought it would affect her more. That it would break her. Damage her. The truth was that she felt no remorse. She had killed Jordan to save her own life and, more importantly, to save Marisol's. Looking at it from that angle, she knew she had done the right thing. She would do it all over again if it meant keeping Marisol alive.

That thought did make her panic. The jacket fell off as she twisted, looking for the woman who had saved her life. The room was darkening, the setting sun cutting oblique orange angles through the pair of high windows and beaming down like a heat lamp over the mattress, making the white sheet jumbled on its surface glow like a flame.

The remains of their dinner of beans and rice, papaya and bottled water had been cleared away while she slept, as had the first aid gear. Packed away in the bag at Sloane's feet, ready for a quick getaway. The green goo had made Sloane skeptical at first, but the way Marisol sighed while she rubbed it into her bruises gave it credence. Marisol had been moving less stiffly even before Sloane had finished. She had used most of the jar, but maybe they could get more before they went to the embassy.

Picking up the jacket, Sloane brought the collar back to her nose. It was a bewitching thing, the scent of Marisol on the jacket. Equal parts softness and strength, just like the woman who wore it. Again Sloane's eyes hungrily scoured the growing darkness. She wouldn't feel safe until Marisol was by her side.

Sloane sighed audibly when she finally spotted Marisol's familiar shape on a stool by the door. Her back was rigid and her gaze fixed on the door, opened a crack to peer through with one eye. Her shoulder leaned against the wall and one boot wedged in place, holding the door open. She held the gun loosely in one hand.

Sloane crossed the room assuredly, her bare feet making no sound on the concrete floor. Still, when she approached, Marisol's head turned to look at her over one shoulder. Sloane looked into her eye and felt her world peeling slowly, gently apart.

"I didn't want to wake you," Marisol said, her voice pitched low in the quiet evening. "Help is coming, but it'll be a few more hours."

Dimly Sloane remembered Marisol's heated phone call on the burner cell. Whoever was coming to collect them was moving slower than Marisol wanted. Sloane should have felt the noose tightening around her neck, but she didn't. All she felt was how those eyes made her knees weak.

"We have to lie low a little longer," Marisol was saying in her voice like honeyed whiskey. "You should lie down. The mattress is clean enough. Get some rest. I'll keep watch."

Sloane didn't respond. She knew she didn't have to from the way Marisol was babbling and how her eyes shined. Instead, she reached out and took Marisol's hand. She raised Marisol's cold fingers and pressed a kiss against them, noting their silkiness despite the callouses. Marisol allowed herself to be led across the room without protest.

Stopping at the foot of the mattress, just outside the pool of light from the skylight overhead, Sloane looked into Marisol's eyes for a long, still moment. She searched them wordlessly, looking for what used to make her detest this woman so much. What made her want, more than anything else, to take her down.

It was gone. There was nothing there but a woman who allowed herself to be tortured to protect vulnerable women. There was nothing but a woman who had risked everything for justice. A woman who was the embodiment of everything Sloane found honorable and good. But that wasn't why she looked into Marisol's eyes now. She wasn't thinking about the spy or the renegade. She was thinking about the woman. The beautiful woman who was so flawed yet so perfect.

She reached forward, taking the hem of Marisol's T-shirt between trembling fingers. They did not break eye contact until the shirt coming off blocked Marisol's face. Even that heartbeat of a separation was agony for Sloane.

When Sloane was dressing Marisol's chest wounds earlier, she had studiously kept her eyes on her task. She hadn't let them stray to the pale blue bra that pushed Marisol's moderate chest into enticing cleavage. The first time Sloane had been a nurse—this time she would be a lover. This time she would devour every inch of The Queen of Humboldt with her eyes, then her mouth, then her entire body.

Sloane reached out and unbuckled Marisol's belt. She was close enough now to hear the hitch in Marisol's breathing, or maybe it was her own breathing she was hearing, expectant and unsteady. When the button and zipper were unfastened, Sloane lowered herself to her knees. Her fingers trembled and she fumbled the laces and straps of Marisol's boots until they were loose enough for Marisol to kick off.

While she pressed the tight leather down over bony hips, Marisol slipped her bra off. Just like that, she stood naked before Sloane. Everything inside Sloane wanted to reach out and touch. The bruises marring that beautiful flesh had coronas of green that could have been healing or could have been the remnants of the paste. The cuts were repairing.

Sloane's eyes devoured Marisol. From her square jaw and broad shoulders, across the points of her prominent collarbones. She had small, perfect breasts that made Sloane's mouth water. Her skin glowed bronze and gold in the sunset. Her abdomen and arms rippled with a musculature Sloane could never hope to attain. In the years that had passed since she'd last seen this body, not an inch of flesh had changed. Her lovers before and since Marisol had all been on the feminine side, but she saw again the attraction of an athletic woman's frame. Marisol did not waver under her inspection, nor did she preen, she merely stood and allowed herself to be studied. Sloane's eyes drifted lower until she could no longer stand still.

Sloane turned her back, closing her eyes as Marisol tugged the tiny zipper at the base of her neck. The simple sound of teeth releasing as she unzipped was earth-shatteringly loud. When the cooling twilight air touched her skin, her breathing faltered.

Lips seared into the flesh of her neck and Sloane gasped. The lips pressed higher and she tilted her head to allow full access. Marisol's fingers slipped under the fabric at her shoulders, sliding it loose, unhooking her bra in the same fluid motion. It fell freely away from her now completely bare torso, catching at her wide hips.

Slowly, sensuously, Marisol's arms wrapped around Sloane's body. Everywhere her fingertips grazed was left bare of skin and nerves. Sloane shivered as she was stripped to nothing but desire. When she thought those hands would settle on her aching breasts, they veered off course, sliding down her fleshy sides to the fabric bunched at her hips. With a flick of her wrist, she loosened the dress and it fluttered to the ground.

Marisol pressed the length of her body against Sloane's back and groaned. Simultaneously, she sunk her teeth firmly into the base of Sloane's neck, smothering the sound she made until it became a growl reverberating through flesh. It was animalistic. Intoxicating in a way that made Sloane's mind go completely blank and her knees wobble. With the first hint of movement, Marisol released her, but there was an unmistakable edge of discontent in doing so.

Silently and gently, Sloane pressed a hand into Marisol's shoulder, backing her up to the mattress and then down on top of it. Without protest, Marisol slid back to lie flat on the sheet. For one heart-stopping moment, Sloane lost her nerve. Her body urged her forward and her mind was just as eager, but she had a flicker of doubt. Not doubt of the woman lying before her, but of herself. Doubt that she could provide what her lover needed. Doubt that she could control her own body. Doubt of everything she had ever done to bring her to this moment. Looking into those brown eyes, melting into the dying light, the doubt evaporated.

Lowering herself to hands and knees on the lumpy mattress, Sloane crawled down the length of the sinewy, broken body beneath her. She felt the heat radiating off Marisol's skin. She stopped, straddling Marisol's hips. Marisol's eyelids flickered shut. Her hands slid across the pale skin of Sloane's thighs, trying to draw her closer still.

Sloane bent at the waist, leaning forward until she hovered inches away from those full lips. She ran one long, manicured nail across the square jaw, letting it come to settle on Marisol's lower lip. The split that had been there the last time they kissed was healing, the skin fresh and pink and fragile. Sloane gingerly pressed her lips to the spot, tasting the newness of the flesh.

Then her need exploded out of her and she couldn't hold her body in check a moment longer. She pushed forward with her whole body, swallowing Marisol's mouth in an aching kiss and tenderly moving her body down into the mattress. Marisol met her kiss with equal passion. Their tongues battled and danced. Their chests heaved in unison, pressing hard nipples into soft flesh. Everything that was real and solid in the world blinked out of existence. Their two bodies, pressed so tightly together, were a single entity.

Sloane forced a hand down between the layers of sweating flesh. Marisol broke the kiss with a shout, tipping her head back, the tendons in her neck straining through her skin. Sloane needed to provide pleasure beyond anything she had ever done before. She took joy in every whimper and every groan Marisol whispered into the night. It was more life giving that the blood that coursed through her veins or the oxygen that inflated her lungs. It was everything. It was Marisol.

The scream that tore through Marisol's throat was louder, more guttural, more intense than anything Sloane had ever heard and it sounded equal parts pleasure and pain. The whites of Marisol's eyes showed stark and bright between her hooded lids. Her scream was slow to die, but quick to build again under Sloane's insistent touch. The second time left Marisol panting and spent, the sweat-soaked sheet clinging to her shoulders.

Without warning, Marisol flipped Sloane onto her back and she slipped into paradise, Marisol's weight settling on top of her. Her fiery kisses dotted Sloane's skin. Lips trailed all over her, across her jaw, down her throat and to the swell of her collarbone. Marisol would have continued her journey down, but Sloane stopped her, cupping her jaw and pulling her back up so they were face-to-face.

"Don't go. I want you here. I want to look at you."

Sloane wrapped her arms around Marisol's bruised shoulders, holding her close in the cocoon of her embrace. Running her fingers through the short strands of Marisol's hair, Sloane felt the frayed and lonely threads of her life knitting together. Sloane had spent many nights in the arms of other women. None had made her feel like this. Marisol's bangs, curled by sweat, dropped in front of her eyes. Sloane swept them aside so her eyes could drink their fill.

There was a moment of complete stillness. They looked into each other's eyes, neither seeking nor requesting anything more than this simple moment of peace. After all they'd been through together, after all they'd discovered about the world and each other in the past days, they craved nothing more than stillness. Then, without speaking, they moved together. Sloane's eyelids fluttered closed, shutting out everything except Marisol's touch.

Marisol was surprisingly gentle, holding her as if she were precious and fragile. In that touch, Sloane realized how fragile she really was. It shocked her that Marisol, of all people, would recognize and understand that. The few times she'd allowed herself to imagine what it would be like to be with Marisol again, she had never imagined her to be this tender. Her heart swelled to bursting at the majesty of the woman above her.

Every stroke of her fingers, every press of her lean broken body, every kiss she scattered over Sloane's rapidly heating skin seemed like an eternity. A lifetime of ecstasy that Sloane would lose herself in if she could. It built so fast it was upon her before she had time to prepare and she shattered into a thousand glittering pieces and was put back together again.

Sloane's release was silent. It came in a flow of tears until she finally allowed herself to feel again. She hadn't realized how thick the walls she'd built around herself had been until Marisol stepped through them—not crashing through as Sloane would have expected—but sweeping them aside as though they had never existed.

The walls had been constructed over a lifetime of rigidly held rules and self-denial. Of settling for women who did not make her feel for an instant how this woman made her feel every second. Of forcing her life into a box that, while comfortable, had never been large enough for two. As the waves of pleasure receded, Sloane realized her life would never be the same. There was room for Marisol now.

"Brin?"

Sloane was still crying, but she smiled as she look into the questioning eyes above her. There was doubt there for the first time. She reached out and lay a hand on Marisol's cheek.

"I'm here."

Marisol didn't ask if Sloane was okay. Didn't question her or demand more. She simply slipped to the surface of the mattress behind her and pulled Sloane close, tucking their naked bodies together. A chiseled yet soft arm wrapped around her and Sloane felt herself drifting toward sleep. She felt so safe. As exhaustion overtook her, the sound of Marisol whispering her newly beloved nickname rang in her ears.

CHAPTER TWENTY-SEVEN

"Brin, wake up."

Marisol whispered as close as she could to Sloane's ear, but she worried even that was too much noise. At least she woke without making a sound, her eyes clear as soon as they fixed on Marisol's face.

She leaned back in, cupping her hand over Sloane's ear and speaking in a low voice that was quieter than the sharp hiss of a whisper. "Get dressed. Quick and quiet."

To her credit, Sloane complied unquestioningly. Despite the danger, Marisol found it hard not to watch that pale skin in the moonlight. She still couldn't quite believe what had happened. Even waking up with her arm wrapped around Sloane's naked body was hardly enough to convince her she hadn't dreamed the whole thing. Before she could get too lost in that thought, she had heard again the sound that had woken her.

In the distance, the hum of an idling engine followed by the crunch of rocks under heavy boots. It could have been a villager wandering the town in the middle of the night, or it could have been The Bishop's men. Either way, they had to get out before they were seen. She'd slipped across the room like a shadow. She hadn't seen anyone outside, but the sound was enough. She'd only stopped to grab her clothes and tug them on before she'd woken Sloane. They didn't have much time.

Checking the back door, Marisol saw the path to the tree line was clear. Either the enemy hadn't had time to locate them yet, or they didn't think to cover the back of the workshop. The Bishop obviously didn't have a huge operation here in Bogota. He didn't need one. His reputation was enough. These men were not as well trained as those in the States. If Marisol could take advantage of that, they just might live.

Sloane was dressed and reaching for their bag of supplies but stopped when Marisol shook her head. She had the gun and the burner cell phone. They were close enough to Bogota that they didn't need anything else. The bag would only slow them down and its rattling contents might give away their position.

At her side now, Sloane listened to the few words of instruction Marisol gave her before they slipped noiselessly out into the night. Clouds now blocked the moon, making the trip easier. Sloane kept low and close behind, just like Marisol told her, and they were under the cover of the scrub in moments. Marisol watched the patch of street visible at this oblique angle. A pickup truck stood idling in front of the house. She could pick out the flicker of flashlights from the house's interior. Not a villager out for a stroll after all.

"Head back to the van," Marisol said against Sloane's ear. "I'll be there soon. If I'm not there in an hour, drive to Bogota."

Marisol prepared herself for the argument she saw forming behind Sloane's eyes. Whatever her concern, she said nothing. She nodded once and grabbed Marisol's face, her fingertips clawing into her jaw as she pressed their lips together. Yanking her lips away from Marisol's, Sloane turned and carefully picked her way over the rocky terrain through the trees.

Reeling from the kiss, Marisol watched until Sloane was out of sight, then turned back to the enemy and crept to the front of the property. All thought of Sloane evaporated as she watched the men emerge from the tumbled-down house. There were three, one significantly larger than the other two. Marisol's grip around her Colt tightened at the sight of Hulk and she thrummed with the chance for revenge.

One of the men trotted back to the street and the rumble of the truck's engine choked off. The driver joined the other three, and all of them marched toward the shed. Marisol waited until they conferred at the back door. She slinked behind a tumbled fence just in time to hear Hulk order the driver to stay outside the door and another man to circle the property. He took the last man inside with him.

The driver turned his back to the wind to light a cigarette and Marisol was on him. The cigarette sparked as it bounced against her leather-clad bicep. The lighter made a metallic clink against his boot, but he barely had time to yank at her arm before losing consciousness. She used the hunting knife from his belt to ensure he never regained it.

Leaving him where he fell, she picked up the lighter and peered around the corner. The sentry was facing away from her, wandering along the perimeter. She tossed the lighter nearby and ducked behind the corner, listening to his approach. As he knelt to pick it up she brought the butt of her Colt down on the intersection of his neck and shoulders. She heard his spine pop and he dropped face-first into the dirt. She left his assault rifle but took his knife with her back to the door.

She could hear someone rummaging through the shopping bag at the back of the shop and sincerely hoped it was Hulk. She wanted to take her time with him. Slipping into the shadows, Marisol made her way across the floor. The other man caught sight of her before she could get within reach. As he raised his rifle, she threw the knife. It brought him to his knees, dropping his weapon and pawing at his chest. She reached him before he could recover and whipped her Colt across his cheek. Hearing Hulk shout, she decided speed was more important than silence.

Her bullet removed the man from the equation as Hulk burst out of the office, firing. She dropped and rolled, heading right for him. He couldn't adjust his angle quickly enough and released the trigger as she stopped at his feet. Using her momentum, she drove her boots into his knee, reveling in his roar of pain as it bent backward. When she lifted her Colt, he brought down his rifle to knock it away and the two weapons ended up tangled together, flying off into the corner. Again he was quicker than her and his fist came crashing down into her cheek.

Marisol's vision tilted. Fighting vertigo, she lashed out at his knee again. It was a glancing blow, but she'd done damage the first time and this hit dropped him. As he fell, Marisol fought through her own pain, pushing herself to her knees. Hulk writhed on the ground beside her, gripping his knee as sweat poured down his face. When she looked at him, she saw Jordan's sneer in his contorted features. She was on him before another thought entered her mind.

Leaning all her weight on her forearm, she pressed it across Hulk's massive throat. When he reached for her face she smashed her fist into his jaw. His head wobbled sickeningly and she hit him again. Her vision blanked out and she brought her fist into his face a half dozen times before he went limp. She leaned in harder, watching his bleeding face turn purple. The color reminded her of Ruby's face when she'd emerged from the hotel closet. Of her mother as she'd lain on the kitchen floor. Of Sloane with Jordan's hands wrapped around her throat.

The image of Sloane made her recoil. She pulled her arm away as though it'd been burned. Hulk sucked in a wet, gurgling breath and twitched. Marisol looked at her hands, covered in his blood. She'd almost killed him with those hands. Almost become that john or her father. She'd almost become Jordan.

He didn't move when she climbed off him and ran from the shop, no longer worried how loud her steps were in the night.

CHAPTER TWENTY-EIGHT

Sloane had no watch to keep track of time, but she wouldn't have left for Bogota without Marisol, no matter how long the wait. It felt like an eternity as she sat in the van's passenger seat, her eyes on the path she'd taken through the trees. There was a bottle of water between the seats. They'd left it that afternoon for their drive to the city and, though her parched throat burned, she didn't touch it. Marisol would need it more than her.

A breeze shifted the clouds overhead, revealing the nearly full moon. There was no hint of sun on the horizon, so clearly visible from the top of the Eastern Hills. Hopefully it would be a long time until morning. She and Marisol had only been in the garage a few hours. So much had happened, it felt like days. She returned her eyes to the path but let her mind wander back to the mattress bathed in sunset glow. Had she truly thought the sex they'd shared all those years ago in Chicago was good? It paled in comparison to the ecstasy of this encounter. To Marisol's tenderness and her own burning need. The memories of those nights had twisted to anger after Krone's revelation.

She would not make that mistake again. Nothing anyone said could ever change her mind about Marisol again.

A shadow moved in the trees. Until this moment she hadn't considered the scenario of anyone other than Marisol emerging from the path. As the shadow moved again, she recognized how foolish she'd been. There were no weapons in the vehicle—nothing she could use to defend herself—but if those men had hurt Marisol she wouldn't need them. She would tear them into pieces with her bare hands.

Moonlight flashed off Marisol's pistol a moment before her face emerged into the light. Sloane took a full breath for the first time since she'd left Marisol's side. Catching sight of the expression on her face, Sloane's relief wavered, but she came straight to the van and climbed behind the wheel.

"Is everything… Marisol! Your face."

"What?" she asked, raising a hand to the cut on her cheek. The hand was liberally splattered with blood.

"What happened? Are you hurt?"

Marisol lifted her hands to her eyes, turning them to look at her own palms. Her hands quavered once and then stilled. "Not my blood."

Sloane ripped the top off the water bottle and splashed some on Marisol's hands, using a rag from the glove compartment to wipe off as much blood as she could. It lingered under her fingernails. She didn't trust the rag was clean enough for Marisol's face, so she trickled water down her cheek and wiped it as clean as possible with her fingers.

She didn't ask what'd happened. She wasn't sure she wanted to know. Marisol was alive and with her and that was all that mattered. She'd wanted to stay with her at the shed. Had wanted to help, though she knew there was little she could have done. Mostly, she had wanted to stay at Marisol's side. In the end, she'd made the decision to go and it had been the right one.

The van's gas lasted them out of the mountains, but not much farther. They coasted to a stop after the last of the foothills surrounding Bogota as the sun was just peeking over the mountaintop. Marisol took the keys, purple rabbit's foot still dangling from them, and tossed them deep into the brush. They had miles to walk, but the morning was cool for most of the journey. They kept out of sight of the roads and as many of the houses as they could. Once or twice she spotted a woman carrying food or children, but none of them paid her or Marisol any attention.

The sun had cleared the tallest mountain when they wearily but warily trudged into the outermost fringes of Bogota. Marisol slid the phone from her pocket and dialed from memory. The longer the ringing went unanswered, the darker her expression grew.

"God damn *cabrón*. Answer the… *Carajo! Por qué* I put up with you *güevón*… *Mierda!*"

Sloane assumed she'd called the person who'd take them to safety, and there were a million reasons why he might not answer, but she could only focus on the ominous ones. Marisol fired off a text, then yanked out the SIM card and ground it to dust under the heel of her boot.

"What's wrong?"

"Nothing."

Sloane stopped moving. "Marisol."

"Let's go!"

"Talk to me."

Sloane could see how much she wanted to refuse. Maybe even throw Sloane over her shoulder and run. Instead, she sighed and explained, "We aren't safe here."

"I'm not going anywhere until you tell me what the danger is. We can handle this together."

Marisol growled in frustration as she pulled them into the shadow of a small alley, still dark with the sharp angles of morning sunlight. Sloane allowed herself to be led, determined to get the whole story. Marisol checked both ends of the little alley carefully before relaxing.

"I have a lot of enemies in South America in general and Colombia specifically." No sooner was the explanation out than Marisol checked her escape routes again. "In Bogota I have one very bad enemy surrounded by several smaller ones. This is not a safe place."

"Tell me why."

"I've spent years fighting to stop human trafficking. There are a lot of people who want me out of the way. When I came here with Dominique I…removed a few people from this very neighborhood. And another we'll be moving through soon. You're in danger being here with me."

Marisol slumped against the wall behind Sloane, hopelessness and pain washing over her face.

"Don't you dare suggest sending me away."

"Don't worry," Marisol said, pulling the Colt from the back of her waistband and checking her rounds for the hundredth time. "I'm too selfish for that."

Sloane put a hand on hers, pressing the gun away. "We're almost there. Are you sure you need that?"

"Oh, I'll definitely need it. If not today, soon enough." The old shadow crossed over her eyes. "This is who I am. When you spend enough time in the shadows, you become part of the darkness."

"That isn't who you are."

She allowed herself a moment to wonder if that was really true. She didn't know half of what Marisol had done in her lifetime and she wasn't sure she ever wanted to. None of it mattered as far as Sloane was concerned. She knew all the good she had done and continued to do. It would surely outweigh the bad. There was no sense in arguing the point, not now when their lives were in such danger.

"Maybe not in my soul, but it's who I have to be right now. I need to keep you safe."

Marisol slid the gun back into her waistband and ducked back out into the street. Sloane followed closely behind. She had lost Marisol once—she wasn't letting her go again.

It took several more blocks for Sloane to realize something still wasn't right. "If it's so dangerous, why are we heading deeper in? Isn't the airport outside the city?"

They passed more sleeping houses, fewer residents here rose as early as the people of the mountains. Only the miracle of their early arrival was keeping them hidden now. That advantage would evaporate as the sun rose higher.

"We aren't going to the airport. We're going to the embassy."

"The embassy? I thought your friend was flying in now?"

"He is. I'll make my way to him as soon as I get you to our embassy and safety."

Sloane wrenched her hand out of Marisol's grip as she came up short. "No. Absolutely not."

"We have to go. Move!"

"Not unless you come with me."

Her patience ended, Marisol marched back to Sloane and grabbed her high on her arm, just under her armpit. She didn't grip hard, but she was stronger and her momentum was enough to propel them both forward. She leaned in close as they walked, her eyes scanning every door and window as the buildings they passed went from one story to taller and better maintained.

"Trust me, if I go in there with you it will only spell trouble for both of us."

A man stepped out of his front door, a cigarette dangling from his lips and sleep still in his hair and eyes. When he saw them, he slipped back in the house without a word. Sloane wondered if he was calling one of the enemies Marisol warned her about.

"I won't go unless I know you're safe, too."

"That's not going to happen." Sloane tried to stop again, but Marisol used her hip to nudge her forward. "If anyone in Colombia knew I was at the embassy, they would find a way to get to me. I know too much. Much more than the location of The Hotel. That was only the start. Once Jordan broke me there would have been more questions. I should never have gotten out of that shed alive and they will make sure I never board a plane out of here."

"Then the airport is certainly not safe for you."

"It is if I hurry."

"Then take me with you. I don't need the embassy."

"And how would that look, Governor Sloane? You arriving back in the States with the Queen of Humboldt? It would either blow my cover or ruin your career or both."

"I don't care."

"I do." The streets were wider now. "Illinois needs you and Washington needs me."

"Washington! That's it. We both go to the embassy and they can contact your people."

"I can't contact them. They can't help. That's not the sort of arrangement we have."

"What sort is it then?"

"The sort where they swear they've never heard of me if I get in over my head."

"Plausible deniability."

"*Exactamente.*"

"But you got into this because of them."

"And you got into this because of me. I intend to honor that responsibility even if they don't."

"It isn't fair."

"Nope." Sloane saw the embassy, gleaming white stone and a black wrought iron fence. The edge in Marisol's voice made it clear that, rather than the building, she saw the soldiers outside. "But it would be selfish to jeopardize all the good both of us could do."

"The good I can do," Sloane mumbled.

"What?" Marisol asked, her eyes on the soldiers.

"I'm the Governor of Illinois, Marisol. I have resources. I can help."

"I've got resources, too, Brin, and they don't need legislative approval."

"I can be creative with my resources."

Marisol peeled her eyes off the soldiers and looked at her, her eyes twinkling in the sun. "Are you considering abusing your gubernatorial power?"

"I'm considering doing the right thing in a different way than I have before."

Marisol moved closer to her, their bodies brushing provocatively. "Let's worry about getting out of here first, then we can decide which approach to take."

They were close enough to the embassy now that Marisol slowed to a stop near the mouth of a side street. The reality of her leaving hit Sloane all at once and tears sprang to her eyes before she could stop them. She hated herself for the tears. Hated herself for the yawning loneliness opening in her gut at the thought of taking those last steps alone. Marisol reached out a hand to wipe the tears away. Sloane grabbed her hand and held it in place, pressing her cheek into it.

"I love you, Marisol."

"I love you, too, Brin."

A sob wracked Sloane's body but she knew they didn't have time for this. Marisol didn't have time for this. Safety for Sloane was close enough to touch, but Marisol still had a dangerous journey ahead of her. Still, Sloane selfishly clung to this moment, with Marisol's hand on her cheek and her love so close to the surface. She wanted to live in this moment forever. She pressed her lips to Marisol's palm, feeling her skin one last time.

"We can figure all this out back home," Marisol said, pulling back. "We just have to live that long."

"Come with me." Sloane tried one last time, desperation gripping her though the tears had mercifully stopped.

"I can't."

"Yes you can! You're an American citizen. Any American citizen can walk in there and find safety."

One of the soldiers noticed them, squinting in their direction as he stood at attention. His focus fixed squarely on Marisol, reminding Sloane of her bruised and battered face. She couldn't tell from this distance whether he was concerned or wary, but either reaction brought attention Marisol wouldn't want at the moment.

She laughed sourly. "Sorry babe, you're not dating a citizen. You're dating a criminal."

It took a long moment of silence for Sloane to pry her eyes off the soldier and realize what she'd said. The silence lengthened and she felt the weight of it.

"Scratch that," Marisol said, looking at the toes of her boots and scratching the back of her neck. "You aren't dating anyone at all."

Sloane slid a hand along her jaw, tilting her face up before running her fingers into Marisol's hair. "No, I'm not dating a criminal. I'm dating a spy."

She drew Marisol into a kiss. Not the sort of chaste kiss one would expect on an unfamiliar street in a dangerous city with a pair of heavily armed soldiers watching, but the sort of kiss that left them both panting and craving privacy. Craving a chance to touch each other again. It was a goodbye kiss, but one that made it clear they would see each other again. Sloane drew out of it slowly, dragging Marisol's bottom lip with her for a moment.

"Go," Marisol croaked, then cleared her throat. "Get yourself to safety."

"You too. Please?"

"As fast as I can."

"I'll see you in Chicago," Sloane said, her eyes demanding rather than questioning.

"Yep," Marisol said, looking over her shoulder.

"Hey." Sloane dragged Marisol's face down to look at her. "I'll see you in Chicago."

"You know you will."

Even before she finished the words, Marisol had turned and jogged away. She knew she should go, but she just wanted one more glimpse. When shadows from nearby awnings hid Marisol, Sloane emerged into bright daylight. Wasting no time, she marched across the courtyard to the gate.

"Can I help you ma'am?" one of the soldiers asked. The way his eyes traveled over her reminded her of how she must look after her harrowing weekend. "Are you okay?"

"No, I'm not okay. I'm a United States citizen and I was kidnapped… What day is it?"

"Monday."

"I was kidnapped three days ago." The soldier looked over at his partner, shock clear on both their faces. "I'm in danger. Will you please help me?"

"Of course, ma'am. What's your name?"

"Sabrina Sloane, Governor of Illinois."

"Governor?" The soldier reached out for her shoulder. "Come inside."

Just before she crossed over the threshold of the gate, Sloane turned. She peered into the shadows of the street, looking for any sign of Marisol. She thought she'd heard the pound of boots on pavement, but the street behind her was deserted. She looked for a moment longer, but couldn't see Marisol anywhere. With a smile, she stepped into safety.

CHAPTER TWENTY-NINE

A chill spread through Sloane not long after the Ambassador left. She pulled the blanket tighter around her shoulders, but this cold wasn't something warmth could fix. It was inside her, made worse each time she blinked and one of the many terrible images she'd collected over the last 48 hours flashed in her mind's eye. The spray of blood when the first bullet struck Murphy in the chest. Jordan's face leering over her, her fingers wrapped around Sloane's throat. Marisol's skin, bruised and broken, while she smeared green paste over endless wounds.

"Marisol," Sloane whispered to the empty room.

The sound of her name helped. The cold didn't disappear, but Sloane's teeth weren't chattering anymore. She touched her cracked lips with trembling fingers, remembering the brush of Marisol's against her.

During the interview, Sloane had not mentioned her name once. She had explained that she'd been rescued from the assassin and that she and her rescuer had both been taken captive, but she had left the identity of her rescuer unspoken.

The Ambassador, his incredulity showing plainer on his face the more Sloane spoke, had assumed her rescuer had been one of the officers assigned to her protection and she hadn't corrected him.

"And where is the officer now?" he had asked in a squeaking, hesitant voice.

"We…got separated."

She'd expected more questions. Perhaps even a spluttering refusal to accept such a benign and obviously dubious answer. The Ambassador, a political appointee with no obvious qualifications, clearly had no interest in delving deeper. It was obvious he wanted nothing to do with what would surely become a major international incident. His secretary had entered to whisper in his ear and he followed her out of the room with barely enough time to mutter his apologies. Sloane had been happy to see him go, but rather less happy to be left alone with her thoughts.

They weren't so much thoughts as an endless stream of worries. Hours had passed since she'd last seen Marisol. Plenty of time for her to cross Bogota on foot and board an airplane. If the plane had arrived. If she hadn't been stopped by The Bishop's men. If the plane had been allowed to depart carrying a woman with no passport and no documented arrival in the country. If she hadn't collapsed in the heat from her myriad injuries. The last, at least, was less of a concern. Whatever had been in the green paste had obviously been effective. She'd shown little discomfort in the time they'd spent in each other's arms.

Sloane sucked in a breath at the memory, closing her eyes willingly this time, allowing those images and sensations overwhelm her. For ten years she had told herself that Marisol had used her during that wonderful weekend. That Marisol had callously seduced her and had felt nothing for her. She'd hated herself for the way that weekend had snuck into all of her fantasies since. She'd tried to wash it away in the arms of other women and she had failed utterly.

Now she knew she'd been wrong. That Marisol loved her and always had. The revelation made her lightheaded, but it also intensified her fear. How could they possibly make a relationship work? A law-and-order Governor in love with her state's most ruthless gang leader? It was impossible, and yet Sloane had done the impossible before. She had sacrificed and worked and made a career for herself when powerful forces had tried to thwart her. She could put the same determination into her love life. She had to. There was nothing and no one in this world she wanted more than she wanted Marisol and she would find a way to make it work.

The office door opened behind her and Sloane worked to force Marisol from her mind. She slipped her politician mask back in place and turned to face the Ambassador. The man she found smiling back at her could not have been more different from the US Ambassador to Colombia.

"Good evening, Governor Sloane," he said in a rich, low voice. "I've ordered a pot of coffee for us. How do you take it?"

"Cream, no sugar," she responded automatically.

"Me too."

He crossed to the Ambassador's desk and reached beneath the front edge. The electronic device he removed was about the size of a box of paperclips and had a small antenna extending from one side. The man smiled and shook his head, sliding open the back cover and removing a coin battery. Tossing the powerless device on the desktop, he crossed to the bookshelf between the two large windows. He tapped on the spine of three books, the last one giving a distinctly hollow reply. This device was clearly a camera and this battery was larger, but after disabling it the man returned the book to the shelf, this time with the false pages facing out.

"That's better." He propped one leg on the desk and smiled down at her. "No one listening or watching."

Sloane's breath came in short, rapid bursts. She tried hard not to let her fear show, but she had the distinct impression that this man could read her far better than Jordan had been able. If he was one of The Bishop's men, she would never escape. If he could penetrate even the American Embassy, it wouldn't matter anyway. Sloane would never be free from his grip.

The man's eyes flicked over her face and his smile melted. "Forgive me. I've frightened you."

He reached into his breast pocket and Sloane pressed herself back into the chair, waiting for the bullet to hit. She deserved this. After all, she'd killed Jordan. Perhaps The Bishop was justified in sending someone in here to kill her. It wasn't a gun he removed from his pocket, however. It was a badge.

"I don't usually show this to people," he said, flipping the leather wallet open to reveal a bland photograph. "My name is Anderson. I'm with the National Security Agency."

Now her heart was racing for an entirely new reason. She leaned forward in her chair, nearly leaping out of it. "Is she safe? Did you pick M…"

She snapped her teeth shut on the name when he held up an admonishing hand.

"Let's not be too specific." His eyes flicked to the device on the desk, making Sloane wonder if he was sure he'd gotten all of them. "I will say that a certain private aircraft took off from a certain airfield two hours ago. They've left Colombian airspace headed north. We have a mutual friend on board who is none the worse for wear."

Sloane slumped in her chair, letting her head fall back. Closing her eyes she whispered, "Thank god."

"Let's not bring her into this yet."

She opened her eyes to see his smile back in place. It was the sort of smile she was all too familiar with. A calculated smile that hid more than it revealed. She had used the same one every day in the Governor's Mansion and even more often in the State's Attorney's office.

"She's still in danger," Sloane said as the chill returned.

"Yes, she is, and she needs your help."

Sloane looked into his gray eyes and watched them harden. Now that she studied him closer, she saw evidence of his age. Fine crow's feet in the dark skin around his eyes. The whisper of gray in his closely shaven temples. His palms, two shades lighter than backs of his hands, rasped against each other. If he'd been the one to bring Marisol into the fold at the NSA, he must've been at this a long time. Sloane realized with a jolt that she had no idea how long Marisol had been working as a spy. What sort of life expectancy did an undercover operative have anyway? When you cross men like The Bishop, it couldn't be too long.

"What do you need me to do?"

* * *

The ache of pressure in Marisol's ears woke her. She yawned and they popped, though the plane's descent made the pressure build again. She pushed herself upright in her seat, expecting the cuts and bruises covering her body to scream in protest. Only a few did and she touched the nearly empty jar of green paste in her pocket. Maybe she would track down the gas station owner's wife one day and thank her for the miracle drug. She'd have to wait until after she'd sorted The Bishop out, however. Travelling back to Colombia now would be monumentally unwise.

Gray held his phone out and she took it from him. He looked tired and on edge. *And not too pleased with me at the moment,* she thought. The phone displayed an article from the *Chicago Sun-Times* which Marisol read as they landed. It was an interesting read to say the least, full of incredible spin.

Chicago, IL- Three State Police officers assigned to the protection of Governor Sabrina Sloane were found dead in the Gold Coast neighborhood last night. Chicago Police responded to multiple 911 calls reporting gunshots and found the officers outside Governor Sloane's Chicago residence. There are no reported injuries to Governor Sloane who was not home at the time. An investigation into the murders is ongoing.

When the article devolved into background on Brin and her career, Marisol stopped reading. The article was indeed interesting, the angle more impressive than she'd expect from the State of Illinois's press office. And why hadn't the newspaper pressed for more information? Surely they didn't believe a full protective detail was assigned to Brin's empty condo? But then the public had believed far more ludicrous claims from government officials.

"Now can we talk about the situation at Governor's Sloane's place?"

The plane bumped its way down the runway toward the hangar. She jammed her thumb into the power switch and tossed the phone back to Gray.

"No."

He spluttered angrily as she leapt from her seat and waited for the pilot to open the bulkhead door. The drive back to Humboldt was quiet. She had nothing to say and Gray was sulking. She'd come up with a better answer for him, but it would have to wait. Night had fallen over the city by the time they neared home. It wasn't until Gray drove them beneath the metal Puerto Rican flag spanning Division Street that Marisol considered her next move.

Dominque was waiting in her apartment over Club Alhambra. She needed to check in with Washington and strategize their next move against The Bishop. Her cover was blown with him and they'd have to neutralize him soon or risk everything they'd built over the last fifteen years. Then there was The Hotel. No doubt The Bishop's goons had been keeping tabs on her. They'd be watching even more closely now. She needed to check on The Hotel, but it wasn't safe to go there yet.

Then there was Brin. For all her assurances they'd meet again soon, Marisol needed to be sure. Going to watch over Brin's condo would be almost as dangerous as checking on The Hotel though.

"Give me the keys," Marisol growled when Gray killed the engine.

He looked around the alley behind Club Alhambra, his eyes needling into every shadow. The music from inside the club rattled the car windows. "I'll walk you upstairs before I go park it."

She turned on him, a twinge of pain shooting through her neck at the movement. "I said give me the keys, Gray."

"Boss…"

"Now!"

He waited until the echo of her shout died before he slapped them into her hand. Slipping around the car, she watched him disappear through the club's back door. The two guards released the grips of their pistols when they saw him. The door slammed shut and she slid into the driver's seat, taking three long breaths before firing the engine back into life.

She parked the car in a long-term garage near The Concrete Beach and forced herself to walk casually, her hands stuffed into the pockets of her leather jacket. Her Ducati was exactly where she'd left it three days ago, though the helmet had rolled off the seat. She slid it over her head and reveled in the opportunity to see without being seen. She fired up the engine and circled the block until she found an inconspicuous spot that afforded her a view of Brin's front door. Fortunately, the media vans provided ample concealment. The vultures were all just standing around, playing on their phones rather than watching the street, so clearly Brin hadn't landed yet.

Marisol settled more comfortably into the seat, letting her mind wander back while she waited to the taste of Brin's lips. She'd plan her next stop after she saw her love safely home.

Bella Books, Inc.

Women. Books. Even Better Together.

P.O. Box 10543
Tallahassee, FL 32302

Phone: 800-729-4992
www.bellabooks.com